DAYS

TORTURE

Previously published books written by
Cynthia Cluxton

Kicked To The Curb - self published
acquiring the use of Allied Printing in
Huntsville, Alabama (currently out of
print)

Days Of Torture - self published
acquiring the use of Trafford Publishing
in Indianapolis, Indiana

Days of Torture

The Return of Amber

Written by: Cynthia Cluxton

 www.trafford.com

North America & International
toll-free: 1 888 232 4444 (USA & Canada)
phone: 250 383 6864 ♦ fax: 812 355 4082

This story is dedicated to my family and friends.

Special thanks to my husband for his support and for believing in me that I can do whatever I set my mind to do.

Thanks to my father and mother for their care and nurturing me to make me the person that I am today and for always being there for me in my times of sadness or troubles.

I am most thankful to God for giving me the writing ability, strength and courage to attempt to put my thoughts into writing. I give God the praise and glory for anything "good" that anyone might get from reading this story.

It is intended to show that no matter what we may go through in our life, there **is** a higher power than ourselves. And in knowing that; for all things may not go the way we want them to, but if we believe in God and trust him, he will see us through everything. Always know that God has a plan!!!!

Thanks to the readers that have supported me and for their much appreciated comments regarding my works.

With all my love, Cynthia Cluxton

Author's Note

The book "Days of Torture" wasn't intended to have a conclusion, but after reviewing its contents, I felt that I needed to explore the characters and present a follow up of events that would close some doors for Sandra Tucker and her friends, as well as for the readers.

In creating this works "Days of Torture" "The Return of Amber" I decided to make this story the finale. I have other story lines that could carry "Days of Torture" into a multi-sequel, but due to the fact that I have other writings that I am working on, and being pressed for time to get them finished, it is in my judgment to end the story at this time.

For those of you that have read the book "Days of Torture", I hope to reintroduce you to the characters that may have won your heart and to the character or characters that you probably hoped would perish. I wish to refresh your memory of some of the events that took place in the book "Days of Torture". I will make an attempt to put an end to all the horrifying events that may have left you wondering about the characters and their lives following the aftermath of "Days of Torture".

For the readers that have not read the book "Days of Torture", I hope that you enjoy this story "Days of Torture" "The Return of Amber" and hope that after reading it, you will be enthused to pick up a copy of "Days of Torture" to get the full effects of all the horrible events that Sandra Tucker and her friends endured.

It's okay if you get goose bumps up your spine and its okay if you want to cry too!

Cynthia Cluxton

Preface

It all began when Sandra (Sandy) Tucker had searched for a manicure specialist over the internet. Sandy was in desperate need for a replacement, as one of her former employee's had decided to retire.

When it seemed as if Sandy was never going to find a replacement, she found Amber Lynn Newby.

Amber was a young woman at the age of twenty nine. Amber's work references had checked out to be very good. Sandy called Amber on the phone. Amber had sounded very confident while speaking with her and Sandy felt that Amber would do her salon good. Sandy hired Amber over the phone.

Recalling that first day when Amber had came into the salon to begin working for Sandy, Amber didn't appear to be that confident sounding person Sandy had heard over the phone during the initial interview. Amber seemed scared! Something seemed different about Amber! Sandy just couldn't put her finger on it as to why she had this strange feeling about Amber.

Not that it mattered but Amber had looked nothing like Sandy and the other girls working in the salon had had her pictured to look like. Amber was a rather tomboyish looking girl. It wasn't because of

Amber's looks, but somewhere down deep Sandy had had second thoughts about hiring Amber.

Somehow, Sandy knew that God was the one putting doubts in her mind about Amber, but nooooo, Sandy just wouldn't listen! Sandy welcomed Amber with open arms!

In the beginning Amber had worked out really great for the salon. The fact that Amber had done such fantastic work and that everyone loved Amber and that Sandy had even trusted Amber enough to let her move into her home with her was unbelievable.

Sandy had all her whole life been a caring and generous being to anything that had breath. She had no reason to be anything but caring! In her lifetime, especially as a child, Sandy had taken in just about every kind of stray animal there was, and had sometimes regretted it, but taking in Amber was one breathing being she should have never taken in! Her regrets came a little too late!

Sandy had trusted Amber so, that she had even given Amber a small piece of her land and her old childhood home. Doing so eventually caused more problems than Sandy would ever imagine.

Sadly, it would turn out that inside Sandy's old home place was where Amber and Amber's boyfriend, Todd Adams would torture Sandy in ways that no one could ever envision! (Read "Days of Torture" to get the complete story) (Visit www.trafford.com to order a copy)

In the end, Sandy had been left for dead! With an ambulance and a team of paramedics on the scene, would Sandy survive the most horrific torture she had ever experienced in her entire life!

What else would Sandy have to endure if she survives? How would Sandy's past affect her future? Would Sandy's life ever really be normal again or safe?

And what about Sandy's friends! What about Sandy's enemies! What would Sandy's friends possibly have to endure from Amber and what will happen to Todd Adams and Amber Lynn Newby? Will they ever pay for what they have done!

CONTENTS

Chapter One

The Journey Home

My name is Sandra Tucker. My friends call me Sandy. As I take you through a part of the past, present and future of my life, I hope that nobody will **ever** have to experience the torture, the pain and suffering that I have had to go through.

It was a dark and stormy night in Michelle Tennessee where I had been held against my will inside my old childhood home by one of my assailants. The date was February 27th. Two days after my 40th birthday! I had just spent the past few days and nights experiencing the most horrifying time of my life and nobody but my assailants knew where I was.

I felt that I was going to die! I knew that I was going to die! I had been shot in the head with a gun by one of the attackers! I didn't know if it was by luck or not that the other attacker had already fled the scene before the shooting.

The attacker that shot me was someone that I had cared about and had loved and had trusted like a sister. That assailant had left me for dead!

Now all alone, my bloody limp body dangled from chains that had me attached to the inside of a closet wall. I was full of panic and anxiety! I was praying that God wouldn't let me die! I was praying that somehow someone would be looking for me!

As my life was hanging by a thread, my mind was playing back the scenes from the torturous events I had just experienced from my assailants. One being the young girl that I had entrusted my life with. A girl by the name of Amber Lynn Newby. Then there was Amber's boyfriend Todd Adams, the other assailant, whom also had cast out his share of shameful foolish torture on me. Though I didn't want to recall the horrific happenings, my mind just would not rest.

As the time seemed to crawl and I had blacked out a time or two, I finally heard a sound. It was the sound of sirens and the siren's seemed to be getting closer. I then heard the sound of what seemed as if someone was breaking down the door of my old home place where I had been held captive in. Then I could hear foot steps as they seemed to be running up the staircase. I blacked out again!

The next thing I knew was that I was inside an ambulance. I could hear thunder and see the lightning as it would strike so brightly lighting up the inside of the ambulance. The overhead interior light seemed dim compared to the lightning strikes.

While I lay lifeless like on the stretcher inside the ambulance, I was praying that I would make it to the hospital in time! I was praying that I would survive. I knew that my life was in the hands of my God almighty!

The rain was pouring down so hard that it sounded as if the rain was going to come right through the ambulance roof top. The paramedics were working on me in the back of the ambulance to try to keep me alive. The paramedics kept saying "stay with us, hang on Sandy"! We're almost at the hospital!

I could here fear in the voices while the paramedics were speaking. I could feel myself wanting to pass out again. I was fighting so hard to stay awake. I knew if I didn't, I would surely die!

Trying so hard to hang on and not die, I began to look around the inside of the ambulance. I hoped that it would take my mind off of what terrible condition I felt I was in. Swaying my eyes from side to side, I couldn't seem to see with my right eye! I thought that maybe the blood that I had felt running down from my head after being shot might have had it covered. Maybe the blood had clotted over it! My left eye was blurry! It seemed as if I was looking through a spider web with clouds hovering around it!

I'd never been inside an ambulance. As I tried to look around, I thought of how the ambulance resembled a mini hospital.

Trying to focus my eyesight, I saw that there were all kinds of medical machines inside. I could hear noises coming from them. I saw hose like tubing that hung from the interior walls. I saw that some of the tubing was attached to me. I was connected to one of the machines to help me breathe. I knew that something, a hose of some kind was run down my throat. I noticed that inside the ambulance was the sickening smell of a hospital.

I felt sick! Again I felt myself trying to pass out. I wasn't able to tell anyone what I was feeling. I couldn't speak. I was fighting with everything in me to stay awake.

Again, I'd heard the words, stay with us! Stay with us! The fear I'd heard in the voices was still ever so evident! The paramedics were doing everything they knew how to keep me alive.

I was in and out of consciousness while in the ambulance. Finally, I knew that we had stopped. Even though my eyesight was blurred, I could see from looking thru the windows of the ambulance that everything was still. The rain and storms had finally stopped. Then the doors of the ambulance from the rear were being opened.

Finally I was being lifted out of the ambulance and being transported inside the hospital. As I was being passed over to the hospital personnel by the paramedics I was still being worked on. I vaguely remember that someone was doing CPR on me. I knew that I was close to dying!

Once again, I felt myself going out. I couldn't fight anymore. I was going to die! I remember closing my eyes and falling into a peaceful sleep. I felt as if I was in a dream mode.

I wasn't sure how much time had passed when I awoke in a huge room where everything was gray. I had not died! I tried to look around. I noticed that I still could only see with my left eye. My vision was still blurred as it had been during the ride in the ambulance. I still had all these tubes going into my arms, head, and down my throat.

I tried to move my body around on the hospital bed that I lay on but I couldn't move! I couldn't feel my body. Oh my God! Was I paralyzed? I couldn't move my hands or feet even though I tried! Had my body been medicated so that I couldn't feel anything! Where was a doctor? I needed some answers! What had happen to me?

Somewhere from outside the huge room I could hear someone talking. I tried to yell for someone to come in the room. I couldn't speak. Not even a whisper came from my mouth. I thought that maybe I couldn't speak because of the tubes that were run down my throat! Surely someone would come soon!

As I lay quietly waiting and hoping for someone to come and tend to me, thoughts started flooding my mind. A vision of Amber danced in my head as I saw her as she pointed a gun toward me. I could hear Amber's voice as she said to me "it'll be too late"! Then I heard the ringing of a gun firing!

What did all this mean? With each thought that came to my mind, another thought would follow. It seemed as if I was watching a horror movie. It was a movie with Amber being the star of the show while I was the co-star.

Suddenly I realized that what I was visioning was everything that had really happened to me! It wasn't a movie! It was real! I had been brutally attacked inside my home as I had stood in my kitchen and then again in my bedroom! I had been forced from my home and taken to my old childhood home place! The place that I had given Amber! Everything that had happened to me was coming back to my mind!

It was there too, inside my childhood home, where the horrific abusive torture continued! It had happened in my childhood home bedroom!

As each scene played out in my mind, I was remembering being burned, stabbed and kicked! Being raped! Being hungry! Being locked in a dark closet! The verbal abuse! Then again, the gun shot! I could hear the sound of the gun firing inside my head! It seemed as if I could feel the bullet as it had struck my head!

Though nothing seemed to be in any order, I had remembered everything that had happened to me! Amber had tried to kill me! Todd had raped me! Both Amber and Todd had tortured me in such a horrifying brutal vengeful manner. But I hadn't done anything to them for them to want revenge!

While I lay all alone in the hospital room, my mind wouldn't stop replaying the horrible events I had been through. Over and over the same scenes flashed in my mind! I wanted to scream for them to stop but I couldn't!

Only for a moment, my mind and thoughts then turned to God. I was thankful that God had rescued me from the terrible trauma. He had made a way for me to escape Todd and Amber's wild violent rage.

Then ever so quickly, my mind went to the voices I had heard just outside the hospital room I was in. The voices had now gotten quiet. I started to feel like I was the only person in the world. I began to wonder if I had died and had gotten stuck somewhere between Heaven and earth! Time seemed to be at a stand still! It was an eerie feeling. I had become a little bit frightened. Was God trying to decide whether to send me to hell or to carry me home with him! But I was saved! I was a born again Christian. I had accepted Christ as my savior when I was a young girl. God wouldn't send me to hell! He promised!

Not soon enough, but finally I heard some commotion outside the room once again. I knew that someone was finally coming into the room. I wasn't stuck in the middle somewhere! I was alive!

With a blurred eye, I saw what I thought to be a doctor approaching with some other medical staff. The doctor came over to my bedside. He looked at me and I saw, through blurred vision, a smile on his face. I was happy to see him! I was happy that I was alive!

The doctor began to speak to me as the other medical staff was hovering over me and checking the tubes and things attached to me. The doctor said good morning Ms. Tucker! He then said I know you can't speak but if you understand what I'm saying blink your eye once.

What did he mean by that! I had two eyes! He said blink your eye! Not eyes! I blinked at the doctors' request. After doing so, I could tell that there was a difference of the way things looked from what I used to look at. I knew then that I couldn't see with my right eye!

The doctor then began to tell me of the damage that had been caused from the gun shot to my head. He told me that it had left me paralyzed from the neck down. He said that my vocal cords were damaged! That was why I wasn't able to speak. He said I had about five percent feeling in my left foot and toes.

The doctor then confirmed what I had already figured out! He said I'd lost my sight in the right eye. I began to feel myself tear up inside. I was partly blind!

The doctor continued to talk. He said I was lucky to be alive. He was telling me that with therapy I might get better. It was no guarantee though! He said I'd probably never walk again!

I was hating this doctor and hating the words that were coming from his mouth! I had never felt so useless in my entire life. I couldn't speak! I couldn't move! I wanted to die! I was wishing that I had of died!

The doctor's voice faded from my hearing as I thought of Jerry Haggard! Jerry was the love of my life! He was my cowboy. He was my favorite country singer! I wanted to know where Jerry was. I needed him! I wanted to ask the doctor to bring Jerry to me. I needed to know if Jerry was at the hospital. I needed to know if he was okay. I wondered had Amber harmed him! I couldn't ask the doctor not one simple question.

The doctor's words somehow found there way back to my ears and when the doctor finished speaking with me about my injuries, he told me that there were some people that wanted to see me. He told me that my guest had been waiting to see me for a long time.

The doctor still speaking, turned and walked from the room and stood just outside the door. I heard the doctor say to someone on the outside of the room not to stress me out. I heard him say that I needed to rest! I heard the doctor say to the people on the outside not to stay to long.

Who did that doctor think he was! It was my hospital room! It was my visitors coming to see me! He had no right! I was angry inside! Once again, not being capable of speaking, much less moving or getting up out of the hospital bed was not going to happen, I couldn't express my feelings.

I watched the door with my one clouded eye. I then saw Jerry. He was headed toward me. Though I couldn't see him very clear, as he got closer, I knew that it was him. The cowboy hat on his head gave away his identity.

Jerry leaned toward my face and kissed me so gently on my cheek. I felt the kiss as his warm lips touched my skin. To my surprise, I had feeling there on my face! I wondered if the doctor knew about that. The doctor had said I had about five percent feeling in my foot and toes but never said anything about my face having any feeling.

I couldn't say anything to Jerry even though I tried! I wanted to tell him how much I loved him and to tell him I felt his kiss. I wanted him to know that I was glad that Amber hadn't hurt him! All I could do was look at him. I stared into his eyes! I hoped he could read my mind as I gazed at him. I think maybe he did! He said he loved me!

Then after a few minutes the hospital room was filled up with people standing wall to wall. Each one had come to my bedside to say how much they had missed me and was glad to see me. They were all happy that I was alive!

Some of the people that were in the room were my employees from my salon Fancy Hair & Manicures! Also among the group of people was my best friend Amelia, and Jamie too, whom used to work for me as a manicure specialist in my salon. Amber had taken Jamie's place when Jamie had left the salon!

At that moment I didn't know if anyone knew that Amber had been the person that had hurt me, and being that I couldn't talk, if Amber had been in the room with everybody, how was I going to warn anyone of Amber being dangerous! I feared the worst that Amber could walk in at any time and I wouldn't be able to do anything about it!

I was very happy to see everyone that had came to visit me and glad to know that Amber hadn't hurt any of them! I was unhappy because I couldn't communicate with anyone.

Following doctor's orders, everyone had came by my bedside to say hi and wished me to recover and then the room had emptied except for Jerry.

Jerry refused to leave. I was glad for that! I didn't want to be alone. Jerry planted himself in a chair next to my bed. As he sat in the chair he leaned up to the bedside rails. Jerry started talking to me. He said I know you have a lot of questions! He said I know you can't ask them so I will try to answer what I think you want to know.

Not knowing if he would understand my way of trying to communicate with him, I blinked my eye at him to let him know I wanted him to tell me everything!

Jerry began telling the details of what he thought had happened. Jerry said the best he could figure was that Amber was the one that had done all the terrible things to me.

I blinked my eye again, telling him yes! Still not knowing if he understood me or realized I was trying to speak with my eye, I didn't know.

Jerry continued to talk. He informed me that Amber hadn't been caught! Jerry told me that the police were looking for Amber. He told me that the police had plenty of evidence to get Amber for attempted murder.

I was swaying my blurry eye back and forth as Jerry spoke of Amber! I was scared to death! I was scared because Amber was still out there somewhere in the world running free and she could easily get to me inside the hospital.

Jerry went on telling me about how I had been in surgery to remove a bullet that had lodged at the top of my spine. He said the surgery had taken several hours. All with success! The bullet was gone from my body! He said we almost lost you Sandy!

Jerry was nearly in tears when he spoke. I could hear it in his voice. He said I don't know what I would have done if I'd lost you!

I blinked at him. I wanted him to know that I understood him! He continued to talk to me and I still wasn't sure if he realized that my blinking of my eye was a means of trying to talk back to him!

He proceeded to tell me that I'd been in the hospital for over two weeks. He said I had been in a comatose state. Everyone had been praying for me, he said!

Jerry told me of things that the doctor had already told me. He said the doctor didn't know if I'd ever walk again. I probably would not! The doctor had told him that I would eventually regain my speaking ability. My eyesight! Jerry told me that the doctors said that there was no fixing it! I would always be legally blind.

I was wanting so badly to be able to talk to Jerry. I wanted to tell him about my fears and concerns. I wanted to tell him that he was right in what he was saying. Amber was the one that had hurt me! I wanted him to know that I loved him.

Jerry told me it was going to take a long time for me to heal! Jerry made a promise to me that he would be with me throughout my recovery. He promised he would never walk away from me. Not even if I didn't totally recover! He would take care of me!

I blinked my eye at him again. I didn't want him to give up his life to take care of me! I didn't want him to feel sorry for me! Jerry didn't seem to understand what I wanted him to know! He just smiled at me and said everything is going to be alright.

I was ready for him to stop talking. I just wanted things to be normal again! I wanted for none of this to have ever happen to me!

I felt myself getting sleepy. I guess Jerry saw that I was. With him still talking, he said to me, you rest now! I'll be right here when you wake up. He was promising me that he wouldn't leave my side. With that assurance, I dozed off as he was speaking.

The next few days and then weeks were a big blur to me. I had been in the hospital for over a month now. I could barely remember waking up from time to time then falling back to sleep.

Then finally one day came that I remember waking and seeing the doctor and Jerry standing at my bedside in my hospital room. I heard the doctor as he was telling Jerry when to bring me back into his office for a check up. I was being released from the hospital.

I saw the doctor leave the room. I watched as Jerry was gathering my belongings and was packing my suitcases. Then I saw a nurse. She came to my bedside. She said Ms. Tucker, are you ready for the outside world? It's time to go home she said?

I still couldn't speak. I blinked my eye to say yes to the nurse. It seemed it didn't matter what I thought or felt! I might as well have been one of the pillows on the bed! The nurse began to raise me up from the bed. Jerry came over to help her. He held me upright as the nurse put a brace around my neck for support. The nurse then put a back brace on my back. I couldn't help them do anything at all.

I wanted so badly to be able to feel something. I wanted to be able to get up out of the bed and walk. Disappointed but grateful, the only place I had any feeling at all was on my face and my left foot and toes and that was only a very slight tingling sensation!

I didn't know how in the world I was going to cope with everything that had happened to me. It just wasn't fair! I had always been so independent. Now I was totally dependent!

It took a while for the nurse and Jerry to get me set to go home. With a brace around my neck and one secured around my back, I was fully dressed from the neck down and my suitcases were filled and closed, finally I was ready to go home.

As I was setting upright on the hospital bed with Jerry holding me up, I saw a wheelchair. It was then that reality hit me. I was paralyzed!

I suddenly felt myself crying inside. Then, though the feeling was light, I felt my tears roll down my cheek. My cries were silent but in my heart they were screaming loudly. I didn't like this situation at all. What was I going to do!

Tears or not, it didn't seem to matter to anyone just what I was feeling! But then how would anyone know what I was feeling. They weren't the one paralyzed! They weren't the one that couldn't speak! They weren't the one that had been through this terrible nightmare!

Jerry nor the nurse seemed to notice my tears. They continued on with getting me ready to leave the hospital room. It took both the nurse and Jerry to lift me off of the hospital bed and place me in the wheelchair. The nurse pushed the chair with me in it out of the room. Jerry walked to the side of the chair carrying the suitcases.

Released from the hospital, the stroll down the halls of the hospital was quiet. All I could hear were the wheels on the wheelchair squeak as I was being pushed to the outside of the hospital.

Finally outside, the outside air felt good to the skin on my face. The sun was shining brightly and the March winds had a coolness that intensified the tingle upon my face. I was wishing that I could feel the cool breeze on my arms or another part of my body and not just my face!

We arrived at Jerry's car. My best friend, Amelia, was in the driver's seat. Amelia had pulled Jerry's vehicle around at the patient discharge pickup area.

Jerry and the nurse lifted me from the wheelchair and put me into the front seat of Jerry's car.

The little simplest things I had taken for granted and my paralysis was becoming a reality quicker than I realized. I couldn't even lift my legs to put my feet over into the car. Someone had to do it for me. I knew from that moment that my life ahead was going to be tough to get through! What was I going to do!

With my belongings loaded into the trunk of the car and I had been buckled in with the seatbelt, Jerry took over the drivers seat and Amelia hopped into the back seat as we headed out onto the roads.

While moving along down the curving road, Amelia and Jerry were talking to each other. They had decided that I would go to Jerry's home over in Trina Alabama and stay with him. I heard Amelia say that she would take turns with the girls from the salon and they each would care for me.

I didn't even have a say as to where I wanted to be, literally, I couldn't speak!!!! I wanted to go home! I wanted to be at my house!

The ride from the hospital to Jerry's place was long and tiring. Though I had been strapped in with the seat belts of the car, all the curving roads had tossed my body from side to side during the trip. Even though I couldn't feel my body, I felt like a rag doll!

Finally we arrived at Jerry's home. Jerry handed Amelia the car keys for her to gather my suitcases and things from the trunk of his car.

Jerry came over to the passenger side of the vehicle to get me out. Even though I weighed about 125 pounds, and that Jerry was a strong and muscular man, it was a struggle for him to lift me by himself. After all, he was trying to lift 125 pounds of dead weight.

Finally he had me in his arms. He had to carry me across his yard and up the steps and into his house. Some of the girls from the salon had greeted Jerry and me at the door.

Everyone was seeming to be so careful around me. As Jerry carried me into his living room, I heard someone say "put her on the couch until her bed is ready". I think everyone thought that Jerry was going to break me.

Jerry placed me onto his sofa. Everyone was making a fuss over what to do and who would do what and when! I didn't like being fussed over. I wanted to do things for myself as I always had done. God, I prayed, why had this happened to me?

It wasn't but a short time, but seemed like a life time that had passed by that I was being carried into a bedroom and placed into a bed. Amelia had fluffed my pillow as my head was placed onto it. The cover was pulled up to my neck. I felt like I was smothering! I couldn't tell nobody what I was feeling! I would have to deal with the smothering feeling!

When Amelia thought she had me all comfortable and warm, she left the room. I watched as my carrier, Jerry, then left the room. I was all alone.

At some point I had fallen asleep. When I awoke, Jerry was setting in a chair beside the bed. I didn't know if he had been by my side the whole time that I had been in the room sleeping but I was glad that he was there when I awoke!

Just as I had awakened, Jerry had said to me, hey sleepy head, I bet you are hungry? I was starving! I blinked my eye to say yes but still not knowing if Jerry had understood me.

Jerry reached for a bowl and a glass and lifted it so that I could see it. Jerry had brought me some chicken soup and a glass of milk. The soup smelled really good! I then saw that he had brought crackers to go with the soup! I began to get antsy! I didn't want the crackers! I didn't want milk! How could I tell Jerry that I had went for milk the night that all the things began happening! And the crackers; oh my God, No!

I attempted to blink and sway my eyes and had even tried to nod my head in an attempt to tell Jerry that I didn't want what he was offering me for food!

Thankfully, Jerry finally saw that I was refusing the milk when he put it up to me to drink. I was trying to spit it back away from me! He didn't force it on me! He put the milk aside. Then he tried the crackers! He realized that I didn't want the crackers when a tear rolled down my cheek and I refused to open my mouth for them! He put the crackers aside.

With the excitement of my actions of my eye movement, and refusing his gesture of feeding me, it was at this time that Jerry finally realized that I had been trying to speak to him with my eyes. After some verbal communication from his lips to my ears, he finally understood me when I blinked my eye!

He ask if I wanted the chicken soup and suggested for me to answer yes by blinking my eye once and two blinks for no. One blink of my eye confirmed to Jerry that the soup was a yes for me.

Jerry fed me the chicken soup like you would feed a baby. God I hated this! I wanted to do for myself! I appreciated everything that everyone was doing and had done for me but why did it have to be like this?

I felt angry inside. I was mad at God! Why hadn't God protected me! Why had God allowed Amber to destroy my life like this! I couldn't tell anybody the way I felt! I couldn't tell anyone anything! I wasn't happy with only being able to communicate with a blink of my eye!

Finally feeling full, I had eaten all the soup that Jerry had fed me. He had taken the empty soup bowl to the kitchen along with the crackers and glass of milk and had then returned to my bedside to sit with me.

The room was quiet. Amelia had come into the room to sit with Jerry. They were just sitting and watching me. I guess around ten minutes had passed since eating the soup. Then I smelled an awful smell. I couldn't question anyone about the smell. I thought someone had farted or crapped!

I then saw that Amelia had gotten up from her seat and was at my bedside. She was doing something to me. I didn't feel anything but I could see her down toward my stomach. I couldn't ask what she was doing! I could only watch her through my blurry eye.

After a couple of minutes I saw that Amelia had a plastic like bag in her hand. I knew what it was! Oh God, I didn't even know when I had to use the bathroom. I was the one that had crapped! I was having to use a bag that had been surgically attached to me so that my waste could exit out from my body. Someone would have to check it several times a day and change it when needed. I later find out that being paralyzed plus along with the kicks in the stomach I had received from Amber had damaged my insides. The bag was a must for the time being!

Someone had to care for me as if I was an infant. I was hating my life! Even though I had someone around me nearly every minute of the day, I felt so alone. I felt like I had nothing to live for.

As the days turned into months I had already started my therapy. In the beginning it was a dreadful daily thing, but as time went by, the therapy sessions were less frequent but no less dreadful. I dreaded going because of the fact that someone always had the responsibility to carry me to and from each sessions.

I sometimes felt that I was a burden on my friends. Though nobody ever complained!

My life consisted of hospitals and doctors! Other than that, I was bed stricken for the most part. Every doctor visit or therapy session consisted of the same routine. I would be lifted from my bed by someone and put into the wheel chair that my insurance had paid for and then pushed to the car in it. I would then be lifted again and placed into the car. Then driven to the therapy clinic where I would be lifted from the car and wheeled into the clinic for my treatment. I would then have to go through a series of treatments. Then lifted back to my wheelchair, to the car, back into the house and then back to my bed.

During the therapy treatments, a therapist would lift and bend my legs and arms while I laid flat on my back. Then I would be placed in a body suit that would support my body in an upright standing position over rails that ran along each side of me. Someone would stand behind me to hold me up. My feet would touch the floor as if I was trying to walk. My hands were placed over the top of the rails. To me it seemed useless. After all, I wasn't doing anything for myself! Other people were doing it for me! I wanted to give up so many times!

This same routine over and over, took place during each and every visit. Time had gone by so fast and I wasn't seeing progress. I thought I was a hopeless case. I was sick of it all!

The months passed. A year had gone by! What seemed hopeless was now looking better. At least now I was capable of speaking. I never will forget the first words that came from my mouth. I had been secretly trying to speak while I would be alone in the bedroom, which wasn't very often. I was so desperately wanted to talk but was afraid of how it would sound when and if any sound ever came from my mouth.

Every day when alone, I would attempt to say a word and finally that day came. I mumbled Jerry's name and the word love. Though I knew my words would be hard for anyone to understand what I was saying, I knew what I was saying! I was surprised and happy for myself and could hardly wait for Jerry to hear those two words I had spoken. I knew that he would be happy for me.

Jerry had come to my bedroom where I had just awakened from sleep. As he came to my bedside he asks me if I was hungry or if I needed anything. Like any other time he was expecting a blink or two from my eye. When I spoke the words "love Jerry" though the sound was crackly and low in volume, Jerry stood in shock for a moment.

I repeated those two words again. Jerry began to holler for the ones that were at his home helping him take care of me for that day. They all came running into the room and were questioning Jerry as to what was wrong. Nothing he said, just listen! He then said to me, "Sandy, say to them what you said to me"! He was so excited!

I again repeated the words except that I had said them backwards. I said "Jerry love". Everyone in the room was shocked and happy for me. They all encouraged me to continue in my learning to speak again. Little by little, day by day, my voice was returning! My voice was still crackly sounding and low in volume but you could at least understand the words I would try to say!

Those couple of words turned into many words! I sometimes wondered if the therapist wished I had never regained my speaking ability. I drove the therapist crazy with my questions! I was always questioning them and giving them a fit about my therapy. I would say things like "this was useless", or ask questions like "how long would I have to continue therapy", or why wasn't I getting any better? I think they dreaded seeing me come to therapy as much as I dreaded to go!

At the doctor visits for check ups, the doctor would do his exams. He'd said I had regained a very minimal percentage more of feeling in my left foot. It had been improving a little with each recheck! I thought that it had! I had thought I could feel my toes better than I had in the beginning.

It's strange, but thinking back now, it was that tiny little bit of feeling that I had in my toes that had made it possible for me to call for help that awful night when Amber had shot me in the head with her gun and had left me for dead!

Just to explain the way that I recall of how things had happened that night was like this. Amber had come into the room where she had previously tortured me and I saw that she had my cell phone in her hand. A gun in the other! Amber had stated to me that my friend Amelia had called for me and had left a message.

I watched as Amber threw my cell phone to the floor of the closet and then my attention went back to the gun in her hand. The gun went off and I felt a stinging inside my head. My body had gone limp.

Through blood covered eyes, I saw Amber as she was leaving the room. I quickly thought about my cell phone. I could barely see the phone lying on the floor. I tried to reach for it, but realized that I had no feeling in my hands. It was at that second that I thought I had felt something with my toe of one foot! I thought, hoped that it was the cell phone! I realized that my toe was indeed touching my cell phone, so I tried relentlessly to punch in numbers.

I wasn't sure if I had even dialed a number on the cell phone that night but when I heard it ringing, I prayed that someone would answer. The ringing of the phone had stopped and then I heard a voice saying "I'm coming; I'm coming" then the phone line went dead! The voice I had heard on the cell phone that night was a soft and tender quiet voice. I didn't recognize the voice I had heard.

To this day nobody has made claims on that call! I get chills up my spine when I think of how that call had saved my life. I believe that the voice I'd heard that terrible night was that of a higher power! I believe it was the voice of God! Who else could it have been!

Though I had been rescued from that horrible night, and my physical being had made a small small improvement, my troubles were far from over!

Chapter Two

IN MY DREAMS

The nightmares were horrifying! Even though It had been just over a year when Amber had tortured me and tried to kill me, it seemed as if it were yesterday! I couldn't shake the feeling of knowing that she was still free. She was out there somewhere! She hadn't been caught.

I worried that she would come back to finish me off. I kept having this same dream over and over where Amber would walk up to me with a gun in her hand and shoot me in the heart. I always seemed to wake up just as I would be falling to the ground.

I would have terrible nightmares about the things that Amber had done to me in real life. I always found myself to be held captive into this very dark closet. It was always pitch black. Chains held my body to the closet walls. I could hear the chains rattle in my dreams! The sound seemed so real! I would hear Amber as her footsteps crept up the stairs. I would hear her singing. It was always an unhappy frightening sound as I heard her getting closer and closer to where she held me captive. The closet door would then squeak as it was being opened by Amber. Though for the moment, I never saw her face but I knew that it was Amber who was on the other side of the closed closet door! Suddenly Amber's face would appear in my sight and she would be facing me. It seemed as if she was so close to me that I could feel her breath on my skin. She would begin to kick me over and over again. It seemed as if the kicks were never going to stop!

Sometimes I would awaken from my dreams and there would never be a clear ending. And other times the dreams would continue on and on! Kind of like reading a book, one chapter after another.

In some of the dreams I kept seeing the vision of a hair dryer and curling iron where Amber had burned me all over my body. I would literally smell the burning flesh of my body in my dreams. I would vision Amber as she would pour acid water over my head while I was made to bathe. I could feel the burning and stinging as the acid water ran down onto my face and into my eyes! I could see what looked like steam flowing up from the tub of acid water. But in my dreams I knew that it wasn't steam from the water but it was actually gases from the acid that was in the water!

Most of the dreams were never in any order. I would dream bits and pieces of the things that had taken place back then. I would always awaken in a terrible fright. I would awaken with tears rolling down my face. I could sense my heart beating rapidly. I could feel the pulsation of my heartbeat in my head! I thought I might have a heart attack that it beat so fast!

Always after awakening from my dreams, I had a hard time trying to make myself calm down and make myself realize everything was alright and that in fact that they were only dreams! I had to convince myself that Amber was not any where around.

The never ending dreams wouldn't stop. I would have these horrible dreams about Todd Adams, Amber's boyfriend. Over and over again, I could see him raping me. I could never fight him off in the dreams just as I couldn't fight him off when he had raped me back then while I lay helpless on the closet floor in the bedroom of my old home place!

Just the thought of Todd Adams touching me was so awful. It was that dream that I wished I had of been paralyzed when the rape had really happened! Then I would have never felt Todd's touch inside me. I would have never felt the pain or felt his hands upon my body. He had made me feel so dirty. Sometimes I still feel dirty.

To this day I hadn't even told Jerry about the rape. I didn't even know if the doctor's knew that I had been raped! If the doctor did know about it, the doctor hadn't said anything to me.

When I'd wake up screaming after a dream of Todd raping me, Jerry would come running into the room. He always thought that I had dreamt about

Amber's doings. I just couldn't tell him about what Todd had done! Even though I wanted to, the pain and memories were too much to bear. I was afraid I would lose him. I would think to myself, I'll tell him when the time is right. It seemed as if the time was never going to be right.

Another month had passed. The dreams had gotten so intense. I was having dreams almost every night. The dreams had gotten so bad, that I was afraid to go to sleep. I hadn't slept a night thru in a long while. What little bit of sleep I was getting was what I call cat naps. I had lost so much sleep, that the bags under my eyes had bags under them!

Those short cat naps weren't good for me or Jerry! Jerry was beginning to worry about me. Jerry thought I might need to get some professional help. He didn't have to convince me. I agreed with him!

We didn't let another day go by to get me help. Jerry got on the telephone. He called and set up an appointment for me to go and see a psychiatrist. At the first few visits with the psychiatrist I didn't want to open up. I didn't want to talk about the dreams. I didn't want to talk about what had happen to me. I was too afraid.

It was finally on about the fourth visit that I just burst into tears. I was like a little girl that had gotten lost in the wilderness and nobody could find her and she couldn't find her way out! I felt so stupid and embarrassed! I was a grown woman! I wasn't a child! Why was I acting like one!

While sitting in my wheelchair, in front of the lady psychiatrist, still in a neck and back brace, propped up with pillows at my side to hold me in place, I relived all the things that had happened to me with Amber and Todd. I told the psychiatrist everything!

She listened as I told the story of how I trusted the young woman by the name of Amber Lynn Newby. Of how that young woman had went to desperate lengths to severely torture me! How the young woman had locked me in a closet and had hit and kicked me! I told her about Amber nearly starving me to death. How that same young woman and her bow had put me in a bathtub of scalding hot water that had also contained an acid in the water and had caused burns on top of burns upon my skin.

I told her about how Amber had burned me from head to toe with a hair dryer and a curling iron! Of how I had watched layers of my skin roll up and the flesh smolder and burn. I told her how Amber had repeatedly stabbed me with her nail file! And how Amber had caused me to loose my finger nails! I told her how Amber with no regret, pulled that trigger on the gun and had left me to die!

By this time my tears were streaming profusely down my cheeks as I told the psychiatrist that Amber was the cause for the condition I was in. And that Amber's actions had permanently disfigured my looks and had permanently destroyed my life.

With the tears still rolling down my face, I told the psychiatrist of how the young woman's boyfriend by the name of Todd Adams had included himself in Amber's doings. I told her of when he came to the house and had raped me. I gave her every single detail! I told her about Todd and his part in the adventure of me having to bathe in the acidy water. Of how his hands upon my body when dressing me made me sick to my stomach.

I know I must have cried a million tears as I dumped all of what I had been through into the hands of the psychologist! Everything that had happened was just coming out. I couldn't hold anything back once I had gotten started!

While everything was coming out of my mouth, I was wishing that I had my mother there with me. I was wishing that my mother was still living. I was wishing that I could be that little girl I once was! The little girl that destroyed her mothers brand new mop! The little girl that gave her mother plenty of heartaches but her mother still protected and loved her! My mother would have protected me from the dangers of Amber and Todd. None of this would have ever happened to me! I expressed those thoughts with the psychiatrist too!

My heart was breaking as I was speaking to the psychiatrist. I told the psychiatrist that I wanted Todd and Amber to die for what they had done to me! I ask her was I wrong to think that way! I told the psychiatrist of how they both were still out there. They hadn't been found! I was terrified I told her!

The psychiatrist listened to me until I quit speaking. She then wrapped her arms around me and just held me. She had felt my pain. She truly understood what I had been thru! She was holding me and comforting me and coaxing me to cry it out. Cry, I did! I cried till I couldn't cry anymore!

After spilling my guts out to the psych, she explained that I had done good by opening up and then told me that now she had something she could work with to help me get through the horrible adventure I had experienced.

With the next few visits it had gotten easier to talk with the psychiatrist about the things I had been through but the sessions weren't any less painful for me. With each visit, I had repeated the things I had already told the psychiatrist and had remembered other things along the way.

The day came with this one session when the psychiatrist said I had made great progress and was ready to move forward to the next step. I didn't know what she was speaking about but I had come to trust her and said okay, let's move forward then ask her what the next step was.

The psychiatrist told me the next step was to bring in Jerry. She wanted me to speak freely about everything that had happened to me in front of him! I wasn't ready for that! I was scared to death. I was afraid I would loose him when he heard about the rape.

I knew it wasn't my fault that I had been raped, but I didn't know if Jerry would want to ever be with me after another man had touched me. Jerry knew that I was a virgin. At least I was before I had gotten raped!

Here I was, now a forty one year old woman! I had never been married and was saving myself for the man of my dreams. I had found that man! Jerry Haggard!

How was I going to tell him what had happened? Would he understand? Would he still want me? And it didn't help matters none, since Jerry had always wanted to have sex with me long before all this happened. Yet back then he understood that I wanted to save myself! What was he going to think and feel about me now?

Jerry hadn't even attempted to try and have sex with me since the incident! I didn't know if it was because I was paralyzed or that he just didn't really want me. Just the thought of all this made me dizzy! Being paralyzed, I wasn't even sure if I would ever be capable of having sex. That frightened me.

I felt like Jerry might just be feeling sorry for me and felt that it was his duty to stand besides me until and if I recovered. I didn't want Jerry to feel that way about things. I was terrified to face him but I knew he needed to know about everything. It would help both of us understand each other. I knew that the truth would set you free so to speak but I was praying that Jerry wouldn't want to set me free after hearing what I had to tell him!

Though I was afraid and didn't think I was ready for that next step, the psychiatrist assured me that everything would be fine. She promised she would be with me thru the whole ordeal. I finally agreed to the session.

All too quickly the session with Jerry and myself was taking place. Jerry and I were setting face to face, him on a sofa, and I in my wheelchair, again all propped up, in the psychiatrist office. The psychiatrist was encouraging me to talk.

For what seemed like a long time, there was total silence. The psych told me to take my time and try to relax. There was no relaxing moment for me!

Jerry had even encouraged me to talk to him and was assuring me that everything was going to be alright!

In my mind I didn't think everything was going to be alright. My insides were shaking from fear of losing the only man I had ever loved. Though afraid and worried, I knew that Jerry had to know what had happened! He had to hear it from me. I just didn't know where to start!

Somehow I uttered the words to Jerry "you know that I love you"! He told me yes and that he loved me too! I made an attempt to speak again and all that happened was my lower lip quivered and a tear rolled down my cheek. I made another attempt to speak. Finally I stuttered and fumbled around with words and even I couldn't understand what I was saying. Jerry and the psychiatrist, in a caring and loving way had pushed me to keep trying to talk.

Somehow I found the courage to open my mouth and began speaking. This time my words were somewhat clear and easier to understand. At first I spoke mostly of the things that Amber had done to me. Things that Jerry had already known about.

Jerry listened to me so patiently. I began telling him everything. When I began to speak of the rape, Jerry took his hand and raised it to my mouth. He was saying "sh".

I didn't know if he wanted me to stop talking because he didn't want to hear about the rape or what.

Jerry then began speaking to me as he leaned toward me and put his arms around me and held me so tightly. He said, I already know! He said the doctors had told him. He said the doctor had came to him after they had examined me when I had arrived at the hospital after the incident.

I began to cry. I began to question him and ask why he hadn't said something about it to me. He said he knew that when I got ready to talk about it, I would. He wanted me to heal first. Speaking about the rape was a huge part of me healing he had said.

I then wondered if he knowing about the rape was the reason he hadn't tried anything with me! Was it because he didn't want me in that way after another man had touched me?

Just as that thought had entered my mind, Jerry told me that none of this had changed the way he felt about me! He said he still loved me and wanted me! When I was ready he said!

I wanted so desperately to lift my arms and hold him as he was holding me. In my mind, I tried to, I thought I could will myself to do it, but I couldn't. I still had no use of my body. I told Jerry that I wanted to hug him. He helped me lift my arms and place them around his neck.

I whispered to him that I loved him. He returned those words back to me. The session ended and with time I knew that I was on my way to a full recovery.

Another few months passed. I was making pretty good progress with dealing with the things that had happened to me.

Jerry and I had returned home after another session of my therapy. He had just gotten me settled onto our couch and that's when it happened!

Jerry began to talk to me about marrying him. He told me how much he loved me and that he wanted to take care of me for the rest of his life. He wanted to marry me just the way I was. His love for me was unconditional. He had even gotten down onto his knees and proposed as he professed his love for me.

I knew from the look in his eyes that he was sincere about his proposal. I accepted his proposal but told him that I had some issues that I needed to deal with first. I didn't want to marry Jerry in my condition. I told him I wanted to be able to walk down the isle on my own two feet if any way possible!

Doctors had been wrong before I told him. The doctors can tell me I'll never walk again until they are blue in the face, but I know with the help of God, I will walk again! Jerry said he could and would wait until I was ready! It didn't matter how long it took! He and I had already been together for several years. There was no need to rush things he said. Jerry told me that nothing could change the way he felt about me! Not even if I never did walk again! He wanted to spend the rest of his life with me.

With no wedding date set, Jerry and I vowed to love one another and agreed that our wedding day would one day come.

I knew in my heart that God would allow me to walk again. I just didn't know how soon it would be. I prayed to God every day for his healing of my body and for his help to get me through the struggles of my life. I knew that a miracle was about to happen!

Chapter Three

MOVING FORWARD

It was 5am. The knock on the door startled me. Though I had made good progress dealing with the things I had been through, I was still a bit jumpy ever since the torture from Amber and Todd! I was sometimes scared of my own shadow!

As I set in my wheelchair in the living room, I watched as Jerry answered the door. It was Tammy Jackson from the salon. Tammy had been my right hand for my salon "Fancy Hair & Manicures". She was running my salon for me now that I couldn't be there to run it myself.

When I saw that it was Tammy at the door my jumpiness subsided. She would be my sitter for the day.

As Tammy came into the house, Jerry was about to leave for work. Sadly, Jerry no longer played his music. He had given up his music career to take care of me. He now had a career as an architect. Architecture had been his school trade. I hated it that he had given up something he loved so much. I had begged him not to give up his music, but he repeatedly would tell me that he loved me more than the music. Being on the road would keep him away too much. In a funny way, he convinced me that he needed me!

A little while after Jerry had left for work, I ask Tammy to push my wheelchair out to the porch. I wanted to be alone for a while. I needed to be alone. She did as I ask her. My porch had come to be my only get away place for me to be by myself except for my bedroom. Though I was always frightened to be alone, there were just those times that a person needed their alone time. This was one of those times.

Sitting alone on my porch, it was nearly 6am. It was so peaceful out. Though I could only see with one eye and it was still blurred, I could tell that the October sky was a silvery gray. My imagination enhanced the visions I saw. The sun was coming up over the tree tops. I watched as the clouds would hide the sun and then the sun would reappear. There was a smoky fog hovering above the ground.

I could hear the birds singing all around me as they were in flight and were playing among the tall trees. What a beautiful sound. The different whistles of each bird echoed in my ears. Their sound was as pleasant as a church choir singing praises to God on a Sunday morning.

Somewhere in the distance I could hear a dog barking. I wondered why it was so easy for everyone, including myself, to take such things for granted!

As I sat outside in my wheelchair on the front porch, I looked out across the front lawn. Along the fence row I saw a small squirrel. It seemed to be in search of food. I watched as it would run away from the fence and up the side of a tree that was near and would disappear way up high into the leaves and branches of the tree. Then back down it would go and run back to the fence. I watched as the squirrel made several trips from the fence to the tree. Honestly I really didn't know if the animal I was seeing was a squirrel, but again I used my imagination to play a part in what I was seeing.

I looked back to the sky. The skies color was changing from the silvery gray to a clear blue. The sun was now shining so brightly. The sun's rays seemed to make my eye sting as I looked into it. The fog that had been hovering the ground had now disappeared.

As I watched the early morning pass, my thoughts went from the beautiful things I saw and heard to the horrible things that had happened to me.

With everything that had been taken from me, I wondered how I could still love life. Why hadn't I just given up? Why couldn't I have my independence back?

I wanted to be free like the birds in those trees and the dog barking and the squirrel fending for himself in search for food.

Why had God let me live and be in the situation I was in? Why didn't God just take me home? Why didn't he let me die? Looking back to those days of torture brought tears to my eyes and pain in my heart.

I guess that Tammy must have heard me crying. Maybe she had been keeping her eyes on me from the inside. Maybe she was watching me from the window next to the front door. Whatever the case must have been, Tammy came out to the porch to set with me.

Tammy and I began to talk for a bit. Firstly with her asking me if I was okay. As we talked, I told Tammy that I was having memories of the past. I told her how it was hard to cope with it all.

After telling Tammy about my feelings and of the thoughts going on inside my head, Tammy told me that if she ever ran across Amber that she would kill her! Tammy told me that Amber better hope that the law found her before she did!

Tammy was extremely angry at Amber. I told Tammy not to try to take the law into her hands. I begged her to let the law handle Amber!

Tammy began to say to me, I swear, if I ever... I stopped Tammy from finishing what she was about to say. I said to Tammy, don't go doing anything stupid. You'll just get yourself into trouble!

Tammy wanted Amber to pay for what she had done to me! Back before Amber had taken her rage out on me, Tammy had overlooked Amber and had forgiven her about a cracker incident at the salon, but now she wanted to get even!

Tammy said to me, if only she had listened to her head and not her heart! She said that she should have just stomped Amber's ass in the ground!

Tammy was still just as hot headed as she ever was! She stated to me that Amber would have quit the salon and that I wouldn't be in the shape that I was in if she had just kicked Amber's butt!

I then said to Tammy, you know, even after everything I've gone thru, I still feel a sad sorrowful feeling for Amber. I told Tammy that it was partly my fault for trusting Amber in the first place.

As we continued to talk I told Tammy that I believed that Amber had some major mental problems. Now don't get me wrong, I said to Tammy; I'm still terrified of the thought that Amber will come and finish me off. I told Tammy that I would never forget what Amber had done to me and I hoped and prayed that if and when Amber got caught, she would never be set free to harm another soul.

While we were still in conversation, I thanked Tammy for being my friend and for being there with me. I thanked her for taking care of my salon and thanked her for her kindness.

Tammy had said to me that she hadn't done anything that another wouldn't do and said that there was no reason to thank her. Tammy just didn't realize what it meant to me for her and the others that took care of me and had stood beside me through all of the things I had gone thru.

Being that I was the one that had hired Amber to come work in my salon, I had put everyone in danger. I felt that as long as Amber was running free, all of us were still in danger. I told Tammy of my thoughts about that and told Tammy I wouldn't want anyone to ever go thru what I had gone through with Amber!

For a moment Tammy and I had gotten silent with our conversation. Tammy seemed to be deep in thought just as I was.

Then Tammy looked at me and told me that she had been trying to do some research on Amber. The way she said it was like it was a big secret! She told me she hadn't found anything on Amber as of yet!

Listening to Tammy talk, I knew that Tammy was desperate in wanting to find any information on Amber as to her background. Where she came from? Where she was born? Who her parents were? Anything!

I knew Tammy, and she wasn't going to give up until Amber was caught! I told Tammy, begged her, to stay out of trouble but ask her to keep me informed of anything she might find out! Tammy promised me that she would. I figured that if Tammy found out anything and told me about it, I could detour her from jumping the gun and taking things into her own hands. I sure didn't want Tammy to be hurt by Amber! My thoughts then turned quiet once again. Tammy got quiet.

Tammy and I sat on the porch for a while longer as we both were deep in our own thoughts. I began to get tired. I ask Tammy to take me back into the house. I needed to rest I told her.

Tammy got up from the porch and helped me inside and into my bedroom and then she helped me to get into my bed. Tammy excused herself from the room. She was going to find something to eat for us.

I told her that would be good because I had gotten hungry.

While waiting for food, I had fallen asleep. I started to dream. As usual, the dreams were of Amber. I was re-living the torture in my dreams once again!

I had awakened in a sweat and was screaming for my life when Tammy came running into the room. She tried to comfort me.

I guess all the talk of Amber while on the porch had brought on the dreams. I was again, as usual, scared for my life. Just as I would think I was getting better, something would trigger in my mind and I'd be right back to where I started from. I wondered if I would ever get over this terrible time I had experienced!

The rest of the day was rough to get thru but thankfully Tammy stayed in the room with me. She didn't leave my side except to retrieve my food that she had prepared for me to eat!

I couldn't eat anything. I was sick! I couldn't stop thinking about Amber or Todd. I had all these questions going on in my mind! I wondered if Amber knew where I was. I wondered if Todd was sorry for raping me. I had so many unanswered questions!

I couldn't go back to sleep! I was so afraid to close my eyes! I laid and stared at the clock on the wall. I watched as the hours passed!

It was nearing the time for Jerry to get home from work. I wanted him with me! I was counting the hours, then minutes for his arrival home.

Finally Jerry came home from work. He came to the bedroom where I lay waiting for him. Tammy was still in the room with me when Jerry came in.

Tammy began to tell Jerry of the dreams I had had and how I couldn't sleep or eat. She filled him in on the whole day we had shared.

Before I knew it, it was time for Tammy to leave. Tammy said her goodbyes to Jerry and me, and then she left the house.

Jerry came to the bedside where I lay and he lifted me out of the bed. I had no idea of what he was up to. He put me into my wheelchair and then he pushed me everywhere that he went throughout the house.

While sitting in the wheelchair, I watched him as he prepared our supper. We ate. Well, he ate and I just nibbled at my food that he tried to feed me. I had no appetite. I watched as he picked up some things in the living room. I even sat just outside the bathroom door as he did his thing in there too. Being weird or crazy, I didn't care! I was glad that Jerry never got out of my sight.

Soon it was our bedtime. Like so many other days, I had had enough of this day and wanted to try to forget it. Jerry put me back into bed and tucked me in and then he crawled in beside me. He promised he wouldn't leave my side. He said he would stay awake until I fell asleep.

I guess he did. I slept the night thru. When I awoke, Jerry was still beside me. He was awake. He had been watching me sleep. Just knowing that he was beside me had kept away the bad dreams.

As we lay side by side, I looked toward the window. I could tell it was late in the morning. I looked at the clock hanging on our wall. Jerry was late for work! I had begun to say to him, you'd better get going... He hushed me!

He then reached over to the bedside table for the telephone. He looked at me and said he was staying with me today. He told me that he would take me to my therapy.

The next thing that I knew was that he had called in to work. I heard him say to someone "Sandy wasn't doing to good and he needed to be with her". After he hung up the phone I told him I'd be alright. But he refused to listen to me. His mind was made up.

With me still trying to convince him that I was going to be alright, Jerry had gotten up from our bed and had headed to the kitchen to fix something to eat. I could hear him rattling pans and then I smelled bacon frying.

At some point of the morning while I was lying in bed and waiting on breakfast, I felt a funny twitching in my arms and legs. I thought maybe it was my imagination. Then I felt it again.

I began to holler for Jerry! He came running into the bedroom. He was saying what's wrong! What's wrong!

At first I couldn't say a word to him. My blurry eye was focused on Jerry's appearance. He looked so funny standing there with an apron on and kitchen pot holders on his hands. I was laughing out loud at him when he again said, what's wrong Sandy!

Still with laughter, I told him that I had felt something strange going on with my arms and my legs. Both of them! The right and left side, I said! My laughter had turned to excitement! I told him that it was a strong sensation like I'd never felt before.

Now we were both serious. Jerry came on over closer to the bed. He set down beside me. He placed his hand upon my arm and asks did I feel him touching me. He was lightly pinching my skin.

I screamed with happiness as I told him that I had felt his pinch! He said to me; try to move your hands and feet! I tried! I was moving them! Not much movement but all the same I was moving them! I could feel my legs and feet. I could feel my arms and my hands! It was a tingling sensation like pins sticking me! I was squealing loudly. I was praising God! I was thanking God!

Jerry being just as excited as I was, he immediately went and grabbed the telephone and called the doctors office and excitedly told them what I had just experienced. When he hung up the telephone and had looked toward me, I saw that he looked a bit disappointed as he walked back over to where I lay.

I ask him why he had such a sad face. Then he revealed why. The doctor's had told him to tell me to come on in for my appointment. They told him to tell me not to get my hopes up for that sometimes the body played tricks on you and it could have just been a temporarily thing going on with my body.

I was terribly disappointed when I heard what Jerry had told to me. My doctors don't know everything I told him! I hoped that I could discourage Jerry's sadness even though now I was feeling sadness about what the doctor had told him too.

My doctor's appointment was nearing so Jerry dressed me for the occasion. As I was being dressed, I noticed that I had lost the sensation that I had felt. I didn't dare tell Jerry. I didn't want him to be disappointed any more than he already was.

I had guessed that the doctor was right. It was probably just the body playing tricks on me. I was very saddened and disappointed now!

The time came to head out for my doctor's appointment. Jerry loaded me into the wheelchair and pushed me out to the car. He put me in the passenger seat of the car and buckled me in. We headed for the doctor's office.

The drive seemed so long. Jerry and I were sort of quiet as I guessed our minds were on what the doctor would soon tell us. When we spoke to each other at all it would be about something other than what was or wasn't going on with my body.

We did hold hands while making the trip to the doctor and Jerry did look over and wink at me a couple of times. I guessed that he was trying to reassure me that everything was going to be alright.

We arrived at the doctor's office. I was quickly taken back to the examination room. After some test, the doctor came back into the exam room. I was dreading to hear the results of my test. I just knew that the test was going to be negative. The words from the doctors mouth was a shock.

The doctor said, you were right! You are regaining your ability to feel. The doctor said, if I'd had to bet on you recovering to this stage, I'd lost. He told me that I was a miracle. He told me that I still had a long way to go though.

I was thrilled when I saw the doctor's nurse come with a set of crutches and a walker! I knew that the wheelchair that carried me around would soon be a piece of furniture that collected dust. That was my hopes!

The nurse gave me my going home orders. I listened as she said for me to practice using the walker and crutches as much as I possibly could. She told me to start out slow and then increase my using them as I went along. She said for me to make sure that someone would be close by my side to catch me should I begin to fall. She told me of how a fall could set me back a ways!

I was deliriously happy! I promised the nurse and the doctor that I would follow their orders! Grateful I was! Even though the doctor had given me a percentile of improvement of somewhere around fifteen percent of having my feeling back, and that it may come and go until my body made its adjustments to what was going on, I knew that I was on my way to a full recovery!

Before leaving the doctor's office that day, being curious, I had asked the doctor for his explanation of how the bullet had caused my paralysis. He asks me if I was sure that I wanted to know about it. The doctor knew that on other visits I'd had with him that I had refused to hear the details.

Assuring the doctor that now was the time for me to know what had went on inside my body that night, I listened as the doctor explained. He began to tell me that when the bullet from the gun shot had went into the top right side of my head, it had damaged some of the nerves of my body. Those damaged nerves were the cause of my paralysis. The doctor told me that I would probably never regain complete feeling on the right side of my body. He told me that I may never get any better than I was at the moment. He told me that the damage done from the gun shot should have killed me!

The doctor then told me that I would probably never walk again without the use of crutches! He said I would most likely always require the use of some sort of crutch.

I told the doctor that I intended to prove everyone wrong! He said I hope that you do!

In our conversation, I felt that the doctor wasn't giving me the information I wanted. Again I ask the doctor about the bullet that had entered into my body. I wanted to know exactly what had happened to me. I wanted details!

The doctor didn't think that I was ready to hear what he had to say but I insisted he tell me. I have patient rights I had told him!

He couldn't deny my request after agreeing that I did have my rights. He began again to tell me of how the bullet had went into my head and of the damage it had caused. As I listened to his words, it was almost too much to endure, but duh, I had to ask!

There was no stopping him at this point. No matter how tough it was to hear what he had to tell me, I had to know! The doctor used words that only a doctor could understand in describing the medical issues about my condition. All I understood was that he told me that the bullet had entered into the top front right side of my head! He said that the bullet had shattered the right eye tissue which caused the blindness of the right eye and damage to the left eye and that the bullet had inched its way down my throat and had grazed the vocal chords which had caused me to temporarily loose my speaking ability. The bullet then stuck right at the top of my spine which had caused the paralysis.

The bullet had entered into my head like a spinning top and had bobbled around until it stopped at the top of my spine. All I was thinking was that I was lucky to be alive.

As horrible as it seemed, I could nearly picture the bullet as it was twirling and entering its way into my head. I could almost feel the dulling pain just thinking about it! It seemed to give me a headache!

The doctor changed our conversation to a different matter. One of which was of great interest to me.

The doctor asks me if I was ready to shed the baggie attached to my stomach. He said that everything seemed to appear normal on my insides and he saw no reason for me to keep it, unless I just wanted too!

I was ecstatic! I was more ecstatic when he said he could remove the baggie that very day!

I ask Jerry if he minded hanging around a while longer so that I could get the baggie removed. Jerry didn't mind at all. He was happy too!

The next thing I knew was that I was being transported next door to the out patient surgery hospital. I was getting the bag removed from my stomach!

I hated that thing with a passion. I was glad that I would be able to go to the bathroom like normal people! Well almost! Until I could master the crutches and or the walker, someone would still have to take me to the little girls' room and set me on the toilet!

With this kind of progress in this length of time I knew I was on my way to a complete recovery. Just being able to feel any part of my body and to be capable of using the bathroom was a great blessing.

I had God to thank for that! I was thanking God everyday for every little improvement and every miracle that had happened in my life. I wasn't angry at God anymore! I know that if God hadn't been with me thru all the things I'd been through, I wouldn't have made it this far!

The next few months were tougher than I had expected. With the help of the girls from the salon and my dear friend Amelia and Jerry, I practiced with the crutches and walker every day. Tough or not, I wasn't going to give up! It was terribly painful though!

There were a couple of times that I had nearly fallen when trying to walk with the crutches. I was stubborn and had attempted to try to walk without the help of others and I had almost paid a price. Luckily, each time, someone was close enough that they caught me before I hit the floor. Day by day and week by week I was improving with controlling the crutches and maneuvering the walker around.

After another doctor visit, it showed that I now had about fifty percent of my feeling over my entire body. Again the doctor told me that it was a true miracle! I knew that!

My body felt funny at times. I didn't care. I was glad that I could feel anything. My body hurt but it was better than not feeling anything.

I was regaining my independence. As bad as I use to be to complain about my aching back and feet hurting from standing up in the salon all day, I wished that I could stand on them and complain some more! Except I wouldn't complain! I would be thankful that I had the legs to stand on and that I had the pain I had.

I would be thankful that I could hold someone's hair in my hands and hold my arms up for hours while doing someone's hair cut. I would be happy that I had a job I could do even if it was back breaking. I missed working. I missed my salon!

Tammy and my other salon working girls at Fancy Hair & Manicures salon had been running the place for me since the incident. I wished that I could be there with them to work. I would never complain again about any pain I felt. But I knew that working again would never be a reality. It would never happen.

I had always taken things for granted! I would never take nothing for granted ever again! As thankful as I was for my seemingly fast recovery, I still had a long way to go. Only time would tell what was in store for my life ahead. Would you believe me if I told you that the horror for me and my friends wasn't over yet!

Chapter Four

Signs From The Holy Spirit

It was a February morning. It was my 42nd birthday! It was the second anniversary of my torturous adventure. I'd had so many days of sadness where I'd relived that horrid time in my life, but today seemed to be so much more vivid and intense.

This particular morning, Jerry was still asleep. I had been lying awake beside him for a while. I didn't want to wake him but I was tired of being flat on my back. I needed to be upright.

Though hating to have to awaken Jerry, I managed to coax him awake and ask him if he would help me out of bed. Jerry got up out of bed and helped me into my wheelchair. Sadly, I still had to use it from time to time. It wasn't collecting dust like I had thought it might.

Jerry kissed me good morning and then wished me a happy birthday. He looked so worn out. He was about to stroll me from the bedroom and into the living room but I convinced him to go back to bed. I told him that I would manage to get myself around and would be alright by myself for awhile.

Jerry finally agreed and had settled himself back in bed and I managed to wheel myself into the living room and then into the kitchen next to the kitchen window.

While setting there in my wheelchair, I looked out the window of the kitchen. I don't know what triggered my thoughts but once again, I started thinking back to that day, or should I say, back to those days.

It had been two years. Maybe my birthday being today had triggered the thoughts going on in my mind. But in reality, nothing had to be going on for my mind to think of those horrible times. I just couldn't seem to let go of that horrid time in my life and I wondered if it would ever truly go away! Rarely did a day go by that I wasn't reminded of those days! It still seemed as if it were yesterday.

Sometimes my thoughts would start out with having self pity for myself. Self pity because I couldn't function as a normal person and I didn't look like a normal person. I was thinking about how I was reminded of those days every time that I took a look in the mirror. The visual scars on my face and my body were constant reminders from what had happen to me. I knew that my scars would never go away!

Even though I had gotten many skin grafts done on my face, you could still see the damage that Amber had caused by the acidy waters, the hair drier, the curling iron and the other tools of Amber's choosing.

I would always have those scars to remind me! Just looking in the mirror and only being able to see with the one eye, which wasn't that good anyway, made me sometimes wish that I was totally blind. Then I wouldn't have to see my face at all.

But then I realize that it wouldn't matter if I was blind because I still had a clear vision in my mind about the way I looked and about the things that I had been through. Nothing could ever erase those pictures.

I began to dig myself into a deeper depression as I thought about my disability of not yet being able to lift my arms high enough to comb my hair or to even put on my make up to help try to hide the scars I have.

And even though I now had about seventy five percent of feeling going through my body, I had no strength and sometimes, like at this moment, I had no desire to get better.

My mind continued to ponder as I stared blankly out the kitchen window. I hated the wheelchair that carried my body from place to place even though I rarely used it much anymore! I hated the walker that wasn't doing me much good and I still hadn't mastered the crutches. My thoughts made me wonder if I would ever be able to get that tragic time out of my mind.

While starring out the window my mind started having this strong feeling that Amber was somewhere close by. I kept thinking that she would come back to finish the thing she started. She wanted me to die.

I shivered at the thoughts that were going through my mind. What if Amber was somewhere just outside my window and waiting for the right time to strike? I believed Amber was crazy. I believed she might just do that kind of thing!

I believed that Amber thought of me to be somewhat like her mother. For when she was living at my home with me in Michelle Tennessee, she had been like a rebellious child! There had been times that I had to step in and treat her like a child!

I realize now that Amber didn't like me suggesting anything of her! She had even stated to me once that her mother used to preach to her about her decisions and for me not to butt into her business.

With all of the thoughts of Amber in my head, suddenly I have this strong intense fear come over me. I became frightened! Was something about to happen? It was those gut feelings you get!

Why were all these thoughts flooding me now? They were stronger than they had been in a long time! And just when I thought I was doing better! Was God trying to warn me about something? Was God preparing me once again for something that lay ahead?

My thoughts went back to the time when I had hired Amber to work in my salon. I had prayed that she would do well and that she would work out. I now believe that God was trying to tell me something then. God had put doubt in my mind but I didn't listen.

Maybe all this was just my imagination going crazy! Then I thought maybe all these thoughts were stronger due to the news media broadcasting and updating about the incident! After all, it was the anniversary of the incident. For the past few days the TV news had talked about the crime and had plastered Amber's and Todd's face on the TV screen.

The law enforcement had even put an APB (all points bulletin) out for Amber Lynn Newby and Todd Adams. Two years and nobody had seen or heard from either of them.

My thoughts made me wonder if they'd ever catch them. Amber was wanted for attempted murder and Todd was wanted for rape. They both were also wanted for fleeing from the law among several other criminal offenses.

And as you will later learn, there is so much more that Amber has kept hidden for many years.

As I watched out the window, my horrid thoughts were distracted by a red bird. It was sitting on a branch of a nearby dogwood tree. The red bird was flapping its wings and making noise.

I felt as if the bird was trying to tell me something. I just continued watching the bird. It seemed like that little bird played in that tree for hours but was only minutes. As I was watching the red bird it seemed to have taken my mind away from the past. I was actually feeling at peace. I felt like the red bird was watching me as it played around on the branches of the tree.

Then a thought, a phrase from the bible had come into my mind. I will never leave you! Then in an instant, the red bird flew away.

Again I started to wonder if God was trying to tell me something. Was God using this red bird for his messenger? If so, what was his message? I was great at asking God for and about things, but as for listening and heeding to him, I wasn't so good.

My thoughts then went back to Amber. What if she comes back? What if she succeeds with wanting to kill me?

I began to cry. I couldn't fight back the tears. I prayed for God to take away the thoughts I was having. I didn't want to think anymore. I didn't want Amber to ever come back. I was praying that if she did return to this area, that the authorities would catch her before she could get to me.

I was feeling very strongly about Amber returning. I wondered should I run and hide or should I face what could be coming to me! Why wasn't God telling me what to do? The tears were still coming from my eyes as I prayed to God for his guidance. I couldn't stop crying!

Then suddenly I felt a peace come over me! It was a peaceful calmness like I had never experienced! I can't explain it! It was as if God was telling me not to hide. He was telling me that I wasn't alone. I'd never been! God was with me!

With that kind of spiritual inclination, the true holy spirit of God, I had made up my mind! I said to myself, I'm not letting Amber run my life anymore! I will face whatever I have to face, but I'm taking my life back.

The tears from my eyes just stopped. I knew that God was smiling at me. I felt God's presence all around me. It was real!

Once again, I thought of God's words as when he said "I WILL NEVER LEAVE YOU". I then glanced back out the window and the red bird had returned.

The little red bird looked right at me and flew away again! Only for a second I felt stress and worry again. Then immediately I felt the worry and stress leave my body once again. It was as if the red bird had pulled all of my worries right out the window with him as he flew away.

God, using the red birds help had some how made me realize that everything was going to be alright. I had a choice! I could either be free or stay tied to the past for the rest of my life. I pulled myself away from the window and wheeled myself into the living room. I wanted to be free. I was going to be free!

I then wheeled myself over to the stereo. I wanted to hear music. I struggled to turn the system on but finally music was coming from the speakers. The music was blasting loudly! Again in a struggle, I reached to turn the music down. I wasn't having much success of doing so.

With the loud music blasting, I had awakened Jerry from his sleep! He came running to my rescue and turned down the roaring load music. Now the music was playing softly. It was a slow ballad country song coming from the speakers.

As Jerry stood facing me as I sat in my wheelchair, with him still in his pajamas, he asks me for a dance. I obliged his request.

Jerry stooped his body down toward mine and faced me as he slowly guided the wheelchair to the beat of the music. His eyes were full of love as he stared at me while we danced arm and chair. I hoped that he could see the love I had for him just as I saw the love he had for me.

As I looked into Jerry's eyes, I could tell that he saw me for what was on the inside of me. He was in love with my heart! He didn't see all the scars I carried upon my face and body. It was as if he looked right through them. I knew that my scars didn't matter to him.

The song we were dancing to ended. Another song began to play. Surprisingly it was the song by "Mystic", the song called "Play Crazy". As Mystic's voice echoed from the speakers and she sang, I listened to the words of the song. Though the song reminded me of Amber and of things that had happened, it didn't seem to have an effect on me the way that it had in the past.

Jerry asks me if I wanted him to turn off the music. He knew very well of how and why that song affected me. Amber had sang it on Jerry's stage one night. Though Amber sang it beautifully, always before, just listening to the song in itself and knowing that I was the one that had prompted Amber to sing and had included her within my circle of friends had always been frightening to listen to. The song had always reminded me of Amber whenever I heard it.

For some reason, this time, the song wasn't affecting me that way. I listened to the flowing melody and the words in the song. As Mystic sang out the words:

> play crazy on the radio, so I won't be
> alone and blue like Patsy Cline, back
> in time, I was crazy for loving you...

all I heard was the voice of "Mystic" and of how touching the words in the song were. I told Jerry that it was alright to leave the music on.

With the music playing softly, Jerry wheeled me over next to the sofa then he sat down so that he was beside me. He asks me if I wanted to sit on the sofa but I assured him that I was fine where I was at. Besides I told him that I was wanting to talk to him about my experience while setting at the kitchen window.

After telling Jerry about my visit from God and what I had come to decide to do about myself, he was proud. He told me that he could sense a difference about me. He said he saw it when he had first came into the living room to turn down the music. He and I both knew that I was gonna be alright.

As the days and months pass, things are about as normal as they could be. Our life consisted of Jerry's work away from home and his work of caring for me when he was at home. There were still always doctor visits or therapy for me. Jerry or myself never did anything outside of the home other than those things.

I had made a remarkable improvement on using the crutches. I had been doing great with dealing with the Amber thing. She rarely crossed my mind, but when she did, I was able to brush her memory aside and go on with whatever I was doing. My life was finally turning into something good once again.

With all of the good going on with our lives, Jerry and I had decided to set a date for us to marry. I had wanted us to have a quiet and simple wedding at our home. Jerry wanted me to have a big and beautiful wedding. He wanted me to have memories of something good to hold on to. I did too, but I didn't think I would be up to having such a big to do!

As it would turn out, it was a big to do. What started out to be a small and simple wedding wasn't! Jerry got his way!

We set our wedding date for August 27th. It was soon approaching and I was beginning to get nervous. Not about getting married, but about the planning of the wedding. I was praying that everything would go as it had been planned.

I was thankful that I had the help of my friends and ex co-workers to make the occasion a success. Things got a little crazy and confusing a time or two but for the most part it was fun and I didn't have time to think about Amber while planning for our wedding day. She had never even crossed my mind.

I was so in love with Jerry and I was happy and I was determined that Amber wasn't going to destroy this special time for me. She could go straight to hello!

I was practicing on my crutches so that I would be able to walk on my own two feet when I took that walk down the isle to marry. A stubborn and determined woman could be something to reckon with. I was getting married and nothing was going to stop me now!

Still, even though I had put Amber in the back of my mind somewhere, I knew that there would come a time when I would have to face her again. I would have to face her either by testifying against her in a courtroom or face her in an attempt of her trying to finish me off. Maybe both! That is, if she didn't succeed with killing me!

Chapter Five

Our Wedding Day

It was a beautiful summer evening. The date was August 27th and the temperature was 80* outside. There was an overcast of clouds that shaded the grounds of the Country Club Stables here in Trina Alabama.

The Country Club Stables was the prettiest place you'd ever want for holding a wedding. There were pink and white dogwood trees in full bloom on both sides of the entrance that lead you straight onto the property. Once you got to the end of the dogwood trees you could see acre after acre of land.

The grounds were covered in a grass of the deepest green. There were flowers of every kind and color that were planted all along the grounds.

There were several horses grazing all along a white picket fence row that outlined the stable grounds. Far out to the right were the stables for the horses.

Then you'd see a flowing body of water that looked like a small lake where the water seemed to sparkle. It looked like stars were dancing on top of the water.

Then you could see this huge Chapel where weddings had taken place year after year. The Chapel was an old plank sided building that had always been painted and well maintained inside and out. The windows of the chapel were large in size and were of assorted colored stained glass.

As you entered the Chapel, to your right was a stand that held the guest book for signing. On the wall just above the stand was a picture of Jesus Christ.

From there then you would enter into the seating area for the guest. Attached to the end of each row of seats was an assortment of flowers in the colors of turquoise and yellow. Those colors were the colors Jerry and I had chosen for our wedding. I wanted the atmosphere to have a sense of happiness and brightness. I felt those colors were perfect! Jerry and I chose to have a classy but western style wedding. So much for small and simple! Everything seemed perfect!

Our wedding would begin at 6:00pm. It was now 5:00pm and I was in the bridal chamber with my best friend Amelia and my friend, my right hand for my salon, Tammy. Amelia was to be the one to stand up for me. Tammy would be one of my bride's maids.

As Amelia was helping me to get dressed, Tammy went to take a peek out into the Chapel. Tammy came back and told me of how crowded the Chapel was. The way that she described it, I hoped that there would be enough seating for everyone.

I was getting nervous! Tammy then told me that she had saw Jerry as he was standing with some men that he worked with. She said he sure was a handsome looking man. I already knew that without her telling me. He was so handsome that girls had chased Jerry all his life. When he was in the music business, I figured that I would lose him to some other woman.

Tammy began to describe Jerry as she had seen him in his western tux, cowboy hat and boots! Her description of him was the exact picture that I had envisaged in my mind. I was glad that I was the one that he chose.

I was excited! Jerry and I hadn't seen each other since earlier in the day. We wanted it that way. We wanted to keep some tradition in the wedding plans. I was anxious to see him!

Very quickly with the help of Amelia, and Tammy adding her expertise, I was dressed in my bridal attire.

As I stood on my crutches facing the mirror, I looked at myself. Looking with my blurred eye, I saw that I was wearing a pearl beaded western cut white silk dress with a long train. A small band of turquoise and yellow flowers in my hair with a white veil that would drape over my face.

My shoes were made custom. They were flat heeled to help me to stand upright, and they were a pearly white color and the top of the shoes set just above the ankle (like a brace). The laces of the shoes were an off white color and were laced snuggly to help support my balance. The shoes had the prettiest custom cut western look to them, somewhat like a cowboy boot but fancy.

With me still standing in front of the mirror, one of the girls raised my dress to reveal my garter. The garter was supposed to be my something blue and something new. My turquoise garter was hidden underneath my dress so it didn't matter that it wasn't exactly blue. It was close enough to blue for me!

On my hands was my something old. A pair of silk gloves that had belonged to my mother. The gloves were still like brand new. My mother had only worn them one time. She was always afraid that she might ruin them and they had special meaning for her.

Those gloves were the one thing that my mother had treasured for many years before she died. My father had purchased them from a salesman that had came thru our little country town of Michelle Tennessee. I hadn't even been born yet.

My mother had told me the story of how my father had brought the gloves home one night after he had gotten off from working in the coal mines.

She said that my father had come home on this particular night and as usual he was dirty and black from the remnants of being in the coal mines.

She said as he walked through the door she had seen him with something in his hand. She asks him what he had and he had told her that he had purchased her a gift.

My mother said she commenced to fussing at my father about him spending any money. Especially since he had spent it on her. My father assured to my mother that he hadn't paid what the gloves were worth, so after a bit of fussing, she accepted them.

She said she then fussed to him that he was going to get the black coal dust on the white silk gloves. She was still grumbling at him when she retrieved the gloves from my father's hands. She turned from him with the gloves now in her hands and attempted to shake off any black coal dust that might have gotten on them.

As she started up the stairs to go put the gloves away into her dresser drawer she was still mumbling about how she couldn't believe that my father had spent money they didn't have and the fact that after he spent it, he didn't seem to care about getting the gloves dirty.

She fussed that she did enough hand washing laundry and didn't need to add to her chores....

She said she had gotten about half way up the stairs and had heard my father chuckling with laughter. Little did she know until she turned around to see what my father was laughing about, but she had dropped one of the silk gloves onto the stairway.

Mother told me that she stomped back down to the foot of the stairs and retrieved the glove. Then she looked up at my father and said to him that she was sorry for fussing and thanked him for the gloves.

My mother had realized that without thinking, she had been just as careless with the gloves as my father had been.

My mother later found out that my father had spent a pretty penny for the gloves so she never wore them but on one occasion for fear of damaging them.

She had passed the beautiful silk gloves down to me and they had been stored in my keepsakes chest ever since.

The gloves were my something old but mostly for me they represented a part of my father and mother. I didn't have them to be at my wedding physically but the gloves made me feel as if a part of them were there.

My something borrowed was a fake silver bangle bracelet that belonged to my best friend Amelia. I was surprised that she had kept it for all these years. It was a bracelet that I had found on the side of a country road when I was very young. I had kept it for many years and when I met Amelia and we had became best friends I wanted her to have it so I gave it to her. She had had the bracelet for over twenty years now.

Amelia wanted me to wear the bracelet. She wanted to contribute something for the bridal attire. I had told Amelia that I would be honored to wear it and assured her that I would return it to her soon after the wedding.

While looking into the mirror I noticed that the girls had even decorated my crutches to match the occasion. They were covered in white cloth and lace and a bangle of turquoise and yellow beads were tied to hang from them. My wedding attire was perfect!

While in the bridal chambers you could hear the roar of the guest as they talked to one another in the Chapel. Then it got quiet. I heard music. It was the start of the wedding march song. It was time!

Since I could only see myself thru a blurred eye, I began asking Amelia and Tammy if I looked okay! I hoped that what I had seen in the mirror was truly what I had seen! After Tammy took her hand and brushed my hair from my face, they reassured me and said yes!

Quickly, Amelia and Tammy had set me down into my wheelchair. They grabbed my crutches and placed them along side of me in the chair. They made sure my dress wasn't going to get caught in the wheels of my chair and headed me toward the chapel. We had practiced the route we were to take several times and did it just fine, but for some reason, this time things weren't working out so great.

Tammy was supposed to push me all the way to the chapel door that entered into the isle I would walk down. Amelia was supposed to carry the crutches and help make sure my dress didn't fall from the chair as I was being pushed. It was simple! Nothing was going as planned! Amelia was trying to push the chair. The crutches got placed along side of me in the chair, and they were nearly falling.

Tammy and Amelia were running over each other trying to get the chair to go down the path we were to take. My dress kept falling and nearly hanging in the wheels. The girls were bumping me into the walls and knocking over things that were setting along the walls of the path. We were laughing hysterically about what was happening!

I don't know how but finally I arrived at the entrance. There was a doorman standing there that would open the door for my entrance. He had a funny look about him. I think he thought we were a bunch of crazy women! I know the guest had to hear the noise that we had made getting to the entrance. I was glad that the doors were closed. At least I could take a minute to get myself together without being seen.

With the three of us still giggling, but trying so hard not to, Amelia and Tammy helped me out of my wheelchair and stood me on my feet right in front of the door entrance.

Tammy grabbed up my crutches and helped me to place them under my arms as she was still trying to snicker with laughter. I pleaded with her to stop getting tickled because she was making it harder for me to stop laughing! Finally all the laughter had subsided.

Though I had come along way, I still needed help doing things. Especially on this day. I was a nervous wreck. I questioned my appearance once more. Both of the girls had made sure that everything was still in place on me and again assured me that I was beautiful.

Amelia then slipped inside the doors and took her place at the alter for the ceremony. Tammy followed her.

The wedding march music was still playing as they had finally gotten into their places. Then the song went to the part where the bride is called for her entrance.

The door man opened the double doors for me to make my entrance. He then nodded to me and wished me good luck. I don't know why but I got the urge to laugh again! Attempting to compose myself from still laughing, I took a deep breath as everyone inside the chapel had stood up and they turned to watch me make my entrance.

I began my walk. I took one step. Then another. I was being so careful. As I was concentrating on my walking, it had taken my mind off of the almost disastrous entrance and had finally let my sense of laughter be gone. Though I was in terrible pain, I was determined that I was going to make this walk. I surely didn't want to fall!

With each step that I took, I looked around and I saw all the people who had attended our wedding. They were smiling. Some of our guest had tears of happiness in their eyes. This was the first time for some of our guest to see me walk.

Thru my blurry eye I could see Jerry standing up at the alter waiting for me to join him. Tammy was right! He was handsome. I felt like the luckiest girl in the world.

I counted the steps in my mind as I was slowly approaching the alter. One, two, three... fifteen, sixteen... twenty... thirty... thirty two. A total of 32 steps. I arrived at my destination. Jerry took my hand and we both turned to face the preacher who was to marry us. I was using my crutches to help me stand there, but Jerry was also holding me up at my waist too. Jerry was smiling. I was glowing!

The preacher began. We are gathered here today to join this man and this woman.....Jerry Haggard, do you take Sandra Tucker to be your wife, to love and to cherish.... Jerry said I do! Then I heard the preacher say Sandra Tucker, do you take Jerry Haggard to be your husband, to love and to cherish...I said I do!

Then I heard the preacher say the words "if anyone has any reason that these two should not marry, speak now or forever hold your peace. There was total silence. Then I heard the words I now pronounce you husband and wife. Jerry you can kiss your bride.

The guest began to holler with excitement when Jerry and I kissed. Then Jerry said to me, Mrs. Sandy Haggard, if you'll give me your arm, I will walk with you to the carriage that's awaiting for us outside.

With a crutch under one arm, and Amelia taking the other crutch from me, I gave Jerry my other arm and he and I slowly walked down the isle to exit the ceremony.

I was still in a lot of pain but I tried not to show it. I walked as gracefully as I could with Jerry at my side. We made it to the outside and the sun was still just as bright and warm as it had been when I had first arrived at the Country Club Stables. The outside seemed even more beautiful than before.

We approached the carriage. It was a two horse drawn carriage. It was decorated with our turquoise and yellow wedding colors. Along the side of the carriage was a banner that said "Just Married" and hanging from the back of the carriage were aluminum cans attached with narrow roping so that the cans would drag on the ground.

Jerry lifted me up into his arms and with the help of the carriage driver; they sat me up onto the carriage seat.

Amelia had followed us out to the carriage. She handed Jerry my other crutch that I had left behind with her and he pitched both crutches over into the back of the carriage. Jerry then climbed up onto the carriage and took his seat next to me. He turned to me and again we kissed.

Most of our guest had followed us to the outside and was watching and awaiting our departure. Just as the carriage driver was coaxing the horses to take us to our destination I slowly lifted my hand to wave goodbye to our guest. Our guest returned goodbye waves and was hollering to congratulate us and wished us a fun and adventurous honeymoon.

The horse and carriage took us to our destination where Jerry had a limousine waiting to carry us to the airport. Jerry and I would spend a few days in Hawaii and then we would return to his home, our home, to enjoy a life together we had always wanted and dreamed of.

Sadly, things don't always go the way we plan them. Jerry and I were perfect but I once again had Amber issues that I had to deal with. As time went by I seemed to let Amber take over my life again. There were times that Amber never crossed my mind but when I did think about her and what she had done to me, I would let it swallow me up and I couldn't function.

Though I knew that God had never left my side, I knew that it was me that had turned my back on God and wasn't letting God be in control. I knew that until I got shed of my fear and concerns about Amber I would never be capable of letting myself be complete and whole.

I knew that no matter how much Jerry loved me and I loved him, it wasn't fair to him to have to live the rest of his life dealing with my being afraid. Would our love for one another be strong enough to withstand what was to come in our lives on down the road!

Chapter Six

SALE OF PROPERTY

I and Jerry had been together as husband and wife for several months. Things between us were still going well, except for the times when I fell apart when it came to Amber and Todd. Though Jerry dealt with things better than anyone would or could expect; I knew that inside he was not as strong as he let on to be.

I could tell in his voice when he tried to comfort me that he hated the fact that he couldn't just fix things. He hated that he couldn't take away the hurt and sadness I felt when the memories of Amber and Todd resurfaced.

He hated that he couldn't make me believe that when he told me I was beautiful that he really meant it. I felt like the ugliest person in the whole world. I hated my scared face and body. I hated the scenes that continued to play over and over in my mind. I hated life sometimes. I hated myself! I hated that I was once again struggling with the things that Amber and Todd had done to me. I knew it was hard for Jerry to deal with me whenever I would fall apart.

Due to the fact that I had been tortured in my house that I owned in Michelle Tennessee and in the old home place where I had grown up, I thought that maybe getting rid of the place would help me to bring some kind of closure to all that I had been through. And besides, I had given Amber my childhood home that I had grown up in along with 1/2 acre of the land. I had deeded her that part of the land and I couldn't nor did I want it back.

After talking to Jerry about selling the place, he told me that it was my decision to make and if that was what I wanted to do; he would help me with the process of selling it.

I struggled with trying to make up my mind if I wanted to sale or not. I weighted out the pros and cons. I had so many childhood memories at my home place. My memories of my mother and grandmother. Memories of learning to become a beautician when I had destroyed my mother's only mop. Our Christmas's together. My relationship with friends. Memories of all the stray animals I had taken in and cared for.

Though I had such wonderful memories of growing up in my childhood home and had spent years of nurturing and caring for my adult home, the terrible memories, the severe torture I had experienced inside both places seemed to out weigh the good. The good memories were in my mind and nobody could ever take that away from me.

After a few days of thinking about what to do, I decided that I did want to sale the place. I didn't want anywhere near Amber ever again. Not that she lived in the old home place or that she might ever come back, but just the fact that she now owned something that was once mine. There was no way that I could ever return to my adult home. It would be too close for comfort for me.

I told Jerry that I had made up my mind and was ready to sale the place. He proceeded with putting the place on the market to sale. He ran adds in the news papers classifieds of the "Daily Trina News and Times" and had posted it on his website on the internet.

On the first day that the add came out in the Daily Trina News and Times I saw that Jerry had placed a copy of the paper on our coffee table in our living room. As I sat on the couch, I struggled to retrieve the paper and finally after a few tries I succeeded to reach it.

I reached to the side table and picked up my reading glasses that the doctor had prescribed me. They were a pair of glasses that were special made. They magnified things much more than a normal pair of reading glasses. The glasses made the words in the classified triple the size. I didn't have to strain my one not so good eye with them on.

I began reading the classifieds in the paper. The ad for the sale of the property was listed and I was making sure that it was listed correctly. I trusted Jerry that it was correct but the news papers have been known to make mistakes in their printing.

I wanted to be sure that the telephone number listed was the right number. We had given Jerry's cell # for a contact. My personal cell number was not to be listed. I didn't want to deal with the sale. And though I had an entirely different cell number as to the one that Amber used to know, I was afraid that Amber might try to contact me if she saw the ad.

The ad was correct. That very day Jerry was getting calls like crazy. The add was listed as shown below.

Beautiful 49 and 1/2 acre mini farm. One 3 bedroom brick rancher, dining room, work/computer room, laundry room, 2 full size bath, double garage. Central heat and air. A large exterior barn, perfect for a work shop or small business. A stream where the water runs into a large pond. In ground swimming pool with surrounding deck. Lot's of extra's. Appraised at $375,000.00 will sell for $100,000.00   for info: XXX-XXX-XXXX

Out of all the calls that Jerry had received, the people were interested in the place until they were told about the 1/2 acre and house that was deeded to Amber Lynn Newby.

Everyone around knew who Amber was. They had saw on TV and in the news papers about what had happened back then. Over the years, it had been broadcast everywhere.

Even though more than two and a half years had passed by, seemed nobody had forgotten. The fact that on the last two anniversaries of the incident, the news had shown news updates and had re-aired some of the previous tapings of what had happened back then didn't let anyone forget!

I didn't think nobody would ever want the property. I figured we couldn't of even given it away. That was one of the reasons we had the property listed so cheap.

As the days and then weeks passed I figured that the property up for sale would have to be abandoned. I figured the place would just run down and finally collapse. Then late one evening a call came in about the house. I heard Jerry talking to someone about it. He was on his cell phone as I watched him pacing from the living room to the kitchen. Back and forth! I heard him say to someone that he would meet them at 10:00 am.

After him hanging up with the call, Jerry came walking back into the living room. I was on the couch. He set down beside me.

I ask him who had called. He told me that it was a man by the name of Henry Baker who seemed seriously interested in buying my house and land. He said that he was to meet with Mr. Baker and his wife the next morning. He said that when he told Mr. Baker about Amber and her owning a portion of the land and the old home place nearby, the Baker's had told him that they weren't concerned about the incident that had taken place there or about Amber.

Jerry said that Mr. Baker had told him that he wanted someplace to raise cattle and a place for his children and grandchildren to be able to play and grow up. I began praying that this family would buy the property and not change their minds. I was prepared to give it to them if I had to. I wanted shed of the place pretty bad!

The next morning Jerry got ready to go meet with the Baker family that was interested in the property. He wanted me to go with him. I didn't want to go with him but he convinced me that I should. With Jerry's help I got dressed to go with him.

I wasn't looking forward to going back to the old home place, but I knew I would have to tell the Baker's details of certain things about the house that Jerry didn't know about. The family would need to know about the few little things that needed fixed and about the age of the house and things of that nature.

The house had been closed up for over two and a half years. This would be the first time I'd stepped foot back on that place since the incident.

I knew that the bad feelings of what had happened on that property would flood me like an ocean, but I needed to face it. I was getting better. That's what the psychologist said I needed to do. Face your demons to rid them! Besides that, God promised he would never leave me. God would help me deal with my demons.

Jerry and I got loaded into the car and we headed out for Tennessee. The ride was long and tiring. The closer that we got to the old home place, the more my stomach was churning.

We pulled up into the driveway of my old home. There it was! My house. My land! Where I lived for all of my life up until Amber took it all away! I felt a bit angry inside and that didn't help my churning stomach.

As we entered into the driveway I was thinking to myself that at least I couldn't see the old house that I had given to Amber. There were tall weeds and brush that had grown up all around the place and had it hidden. Even though I couldn't see the old home, just thinking and knowing that it was still standing gave me chills.

Jerry stopped our car just in front of the closed double garage doors of my latter home. The grounds around that place had grown up with tall weeds and brush too. Just as he got the car stopped I began having this feeling like things were going to happen to us. Bad things! I hoped that this family that was coming to see the place wasn't a trick of Amber's to get us out at the old place. Neither Jerry nor myself had thought about Amber that she might try something like that until we had arrived. When I told Jerry of my fear of something like that happening, he assured me that he was keeping his eyes open for anything that might seem suspicious.

As we sat in the car waiting I happen to glance into the mirror on the sun visor of our car. Though my sight was cloudy, I saw that a car had pulled in behind us.

The car behind us had barely gotten stopped when a couple of small children had exited from the rear doors of the car. The children began running around all over the huge grounds and had found my childhood swing. A swing made with an old tire that hung from a rope that hung from an old oak tree. The children were making themselves at home as they took turns pushing each other in the ole tire swing.

My mind then went back to the car that had pulled in behind us. I saw Jerry as he looked over the back seat of our car and was looking at the car behind us. He assured me that he didn't see Amber in the car. Inside the car was an older man and woman and a boy in his early teens.

Jerry opened up his car door and walked toward the visitor's car. He greeted them with a handshake and welcomed them to get out of their car. With all of them out of their car, Mrs. Baker sent the teen to watch out for the younger children. Then with the couple following closely behind Jerry, Jerry came to my side of the car and helped me to get out too.

With Jerry at my side, and believe me when I say at my side, for I was so close to him that a needle wouldn't be able to pass between us, he was helping me walk as we all went to the front entrance of the house. Jerry had tucked my crutches underneath his arm for me to use once we all were inside the house.

Though I believed Jerry when he told me that Amber wasn't any where around and that all was okay, I still was frightened about being at the old home place. I was having uneasy feelings!

Once inside the house my mind was flooded with the bad memories. I began to think about the fact that this is where it all started! This is where Amber had begun her torture on me before she had brutally dragged me to the home that I had given her!

Jerry still at my side, but not as close as before, and my crutches under my arms, and trying not to show how afraid I was, I hurriedly, as fast as my body would allow me, I showed the Bakers the house and told them everything I could remember about the place. I just wanted to get the heck out of there!

Finally back outside and Jerry had helped me back into our car, I felt somewhat safe once again though while I sat in the car waiting for the Baker couple and their children to leave, my insides were shaking! I know that Jerry saw the fear I had while I was inside the house because he quickly made a way for us to escape the couple's friendliness so that he could get me away from the place.

Before we left the driveway, Jerry had told the couple to take a couple of days to think about buying the place before making a final decision and told them to give him a call either way. If Jerry hadn't of been with me and hadn't of gotten me out of there when he did, I couldn't have gotten through this meeting.

Waiting for a phone call from the Baker family was nerve racking. And it didn't help me any that I was still sick to my stomach about the visit at the home place. I prayed to God that the Baker's would want the property. Then I beat myself up just thinking about the fact if they didn't want it!

As it turned out, the family loved the place. They wanted it! Within a couple of days Jerry and I, along with the Bakers had went and got the legal paper work done and it was final. That house and property was out of my life!

As far as the salon "Fancy Hair & Manicures", I decided to sell it also. The girls that had worked for me were all still working at the salon trying to keep it running. They didn't want me to sell, but they understood that it would always be a reminder of those bad times when Amber had worked there for me as a manicurist.

It was there at the salon where that Amber had gained our trust and had caused us to love her. She had caused us all to look over her poor pitiful somewhat strange ways.

Though I was a determined person and had healed greatly, my doctors advised me to never work again. At least not in a field of work where that I would have to stand for long periods of time. Too, the doctors had told me that my hands would never be capable of holding an object for any lengthy time, so I didn't need the salon.

Tammy Jackson ended up with the salon. She'd taken out a business loan and bought everything, which included the property, the building and the salon equipment along with all the supplies. Tammy buying the salon had made it possible for the other girls to keep their jobs at the salon too. It helped that I sold it to her dirt cheap too.

The salon was still the most popular salon around even though we had lost a few clients because of Amber. Some of the biggest names in business visited the salon on a regular basis. The local clients of Brownsboro Tennessee that visited regularly would have hated to see the place closed down! And too, with the salon staying in operation, in a way, Amber had been defeated.

Out of all the celebrity clientele that came to the salon, I was surprised to find out that "Mystic" still came to the salon on a regular bases. I figured that after Mystic's encounter with Amber at the salon, she would never return! (Mystic was one of Amber's first customers on Amber's first day of work at the salon. Mystic had stated to me back then that Amber appeared to be a bit nutsy she called it, but had bragged of Amber's work as she had showed off her nails upon her exiting).

Though Amber was no longer working at the salon, she had caused some of the clientele to go other places to have their hair and or nails done. Amber had hurt so many people in so many ways. Not so much as in a physical way as she had hurt me, but in ways that caused the ex-clientele to loose faith in a place that I had put my whole life's work into. Amber had caused the employee's of the salon to loose tip money due to the loss of clientele. She had caused people in general to not trust others.

Amber had pretty much made the small town of Brownsboro Tennessee into a place that no newcomer would ever want to live. Even some of the residents that had lived in Brownsboro for most of their lives had packed up and moved away. Though they didn't know Amber on a personal basis, they had seen and heard enough about her that they were frightened for their families and themselves. I can't say that I blame them.

As for Mystic, I figured that since she traveled all over the world to do her music and singing, she may have not heard about Amber and what she had done. I figured that Tammy nor none of the others working in the salon had mentioned to Mystic about Amber. They sure didn't need to hurt the salon business any more than it had already been hurt.

As I think of Mystic, I think about the song "Play Crazy" that Mystic had recorded and had made it a hit. I thought about how the song had been out for several years now and to this day it has managed to stay in at least the top forty on the country music charts. That was quite an accomplishment!

Thinking about Mystic and her music then reminded me again of Amber. I thought of how much Amber sounded exactly like Mystic when she sang. I thought of how that Amber could have gone places with her voice and musical talent. Instead, Amber chose a road that would probably lead to her death sooner or later.

Though I hated Amber for all of the trauma she has caused me to go through, I thought it was such a shame that a person with great potential for success had just thrown it all away. Amber could have succeeded in a music career or even in a salon business if she had kept her head together.

With my former home place and the salon no longer any of my concerns I hoped that I could move forward with my life. I hoped that I could put Amber and Todd out of my mind and life completely. In reality, I knew that the only way that I'd ever get over being afraid of Amber was if Amber was finally captured and sentenced to death.

As for Todd Adams, I was afraid of him but not in the same way that I was with Amber. Sure Todd had helped Amber with the acidy bath and he had raped me, but I believed that he would have never helped Amber if she hadn't convinced him that he had to, and for him raping me, I wasn't afraid of him because he would never have the chance to hurt me in that way ever again.

Tammy now owning and running the salon was a pretty big load on her. Thinking that it would give Tammy more free time to tend to the salon, I had told Tammy that I felt that I had improved physically enough that she wouldn't have to come and sit with me anymore. I had told her and the others that I would be fine by myself. None of them listened.

They had asked me how did I think I would be able to get myself in and out of my wheelchair by myself. I could walk once being upright but hadn't built my strength enough to lift myself up from my sitting or lying position. I told them that Jerry could set me in the chair before he left for work each day and that I would stay there until he arrived home. I wasn't thinking about the fact that I might have to go to the bathroom, so I guess I did need them! They continued to come and stay during the days that Jerry worked.

Tammy's day had arrived for her to come over. She and I hung out kind of like we used to when we had our girls sleep over. Except I wasn't yet capable of doing anyone's hair or make-up. Tammy had fixed my hair and had applied my make-up to my face. I wasn't really up to her doing any of that but she had insisted.

Tammy and I ate junk foods all through the day and had watched one of those reality shows on TV. We talked about the old times and of the fun we used to have. All the talk had made me miss our times we spent together. Those days were gone I told Tammy.

Imagine a house full of girls; women; acting like a bunch of teenagers. Having make-up fights like pillow fights, eating popcorn and other junk food, fixing each others hair and doing manicures on each other, watching movies and talking about everything under the sun, staying up nearly all night then crashing anywhere you could find a place to lay your head down. Then the next morning everybody one by one awakened and would find their way into the kitchen only to realize that a big mess had been made and somebody was going to have to clean it up. Everyone would pitch in and start cleaning the mess up all the while acting goofy and crazy. Ah, those were the days!

The girl sleepovers were always held at my home in Michelle Tennessee. Now that I was married and living in a home I shared with Jerry, the sleepover's had just gotten put aside. I know that Jerry wouldn't have cared if all the girls gathered at our home here in Trina Alabama, but with so much that had happened over the past years, a sleepover wasn't in the cards.

As Tammy and I talked and reminisced about the fun times that we had shared, Tammy had somehow gotten on the subject of the salon and then of Mystic. Tammy told me that Mystic had come to the salon not long ago. She said she had told Mystic all about what Amber had done to me. I was right. Mystic being on the road so much hadn't heard what had happened.

Tammy told me that Mystic couldn't believe that the Amber that had done her nails so beautifully was the same Amber that had tortured me, even though she had remembered Amber seeming a little weird, a little nutty back then!

Tammy told me that Mystic was going to give me a call and check on me. Guess what? She did! I got the call from Mystic that very day that Tammy was there sitting with me!

During my conversation with Mystic, she seemed very concerned and had offered her help to me in any way. Mystic was so kind spoken to me. She had even offered to come to my new home and sit with me if Jerry needed her to. I thanked her for her generous offer but declined. Mystic had a full plate already with her work schedule. She didn't need nothing else added to her work load.

Mystic and I spoke for a long period of time when she had called. While talking to her I felt as if Mystic thought of me as one of her close friends or even a part of her family. She seemed like family to me too. I needed that kind of closeness. I didn't have any family left except for Jerry. Mystic and I hated that our conversation had to end so soon but Mystic had to hang up and get ready to hit the road/stage once again.

I knew all about the road stuff. Jerry had played music on the road for many years and we had had many of our conversations to be ended because of a time line that he had to meet. That's the way that kind of life is. You never really knew where you might end up!

Anyway, Mystic and I said goodbye and ended our conversation. Mystic had assured me that she would keep in contact with me and promised to keep me in her prayers. I knew she would!

I hang up the telephone and Tammy and I talk again about Mystic and other things. Tammy eats more junk food. Not me, I am stuffed! I nap for awhile as Tammy sits and looks at a magazine. Jerry arrives home and Tammy takes off to tend to her salon.

A couple of months go by. Tammy and I once again share a day of fun. I learned that Tammy was doing great things with the salon. She had made some changes. She had remodeled the salon. She had shown me pictures of the newly renovated salon. It didn't look anything at all like the salon had looked when I owned it. The change was good. Tammy told me that the changes had helped all of them not to think so much about Amber. They were having a hard time with the Amber thing too.

I recall telling Tammy that with time, Amber would just be a thing of the past. At least that's how I was trying to look at it. That's when Tammy had reminded me that she hadn't given up on her research of trying to find out anything she could about Amber's past. She hadn't found anything on her yet. It was as if Amber had disappeared off the face of the earth! Nobody seemed to know anything about Amber and nobody could find Amber!

Soon another year passes. Every now and then, I'd get a letter from the family that bought the old home place where I once lived. They had written to me that they loved the house. Their children loved it.

They had described to me in their letters of how the children had so much space to run around and play. The old tire swing was still hanging from the tree and the children still swung on it though the rope was getting thin and needed replaced. The family had enough land to ride their horses. They had enough land to raise their cows, pigs and chickens. They had written to tell me that the place was perfect for them.

They had written that the place was truly a country setting with all the city conveniences just like I had told them! They wrote and told me that the city had since annexed and now the nearest grocery store was only 10 minutes away.

That was a big difference from the 10 miles I once traveled to go grocery shopping for small things and I had to drive 50 miles to a major grocery store that stocked anything I needed. They wrote and told that there was now a gas station only 4 miles away. They had wrote and told me that things were really expanding all around the place. They only hoped it wouldn't expand and get any closer to them!

They had written and told me that they couldn't thank me enough for selling them that property. They said they had planted a huge garden. They wrote saying for me to come by sometimes. They said they would load me down with veggies from the garden.

While reading their letter, I could tell that they were some real nice folks. It was nice of them to be so kind, but they didn't realize how that place still affected me. I couldn't return there. Being there for the showing of the house that day was hard enough.

One afternoon when Jerry had came home from work, I told him about the new owners of my old home place sending another letter. I told him about their kindness and I read their letter to him. My reading ability wasn't the best that it should be but I was coming along better than I ever thought I would. Reading was good for me. My therapist and doctors had told me to read as much as I could. It would help me heal they said. I would read my Bible daily. That was my best medicine.

Though my body had made a remarkable recovery, I was still having to use the wheelchair from time to time. The dust hadn't settled on it yet! And not being able to stand for very long and still having limited use of my body didn't leave me with much more that I could do other than to read. Not that I didn't try though. I was never going to give up!

When a person goes from being totally independent and then having to be dependent on another makes it hard to cope. However, on my good days, among the things I could do or tried to do was that I could wheel myself around in the wheelchair and pick up a magazine from a table or dust around things within my reach and even then those small chores were a struggle sometimes.

The walker that had not been of much use before was now a big part of my getting my independence back. Though most times someone would still have to help me to get up from my wheelchair and place me up to the walker, once upright and standing, I was able to go around inside the house for very short walks. I used the walker and my crutches as much as possible. I wanted to get stronger. I wanted to walk again without the help of any crutch!

I have wondered how that I managed to make that walk down the isle when Jerry and I married. But then I recall that I was in an awful lot of pain then! Being that I was determined to make that walk and the motivation and adrenaline that I had going on at the time had helped. It was kind of like my body had taken a brief setback.

I was real good with the remote for the TV. I would set there in my wheel chair and watch TV for hours on end. Why, I don't know? It was always so much bad news on the TV. Every time you turn around, it was someone killed, robbed, abused or something. I guess in some way it made me feel better to know that I wasn't the only person in the world that had gone thru bad times, even though sometimes I felt like I was.

I was still so dependent on Jerry. I wondered sometimes how long he'd continue to be there for me. He had given up so much to take care of me. His music! That used to be his whole life!

After reading the letter to Jerry, I became tired; I fell asleep in the wheelchair as I was reading to him. I must have been in a deep sleep. For when I awoke, I was in my bed all tucked in. Jerry was up and dressed for work. I had slept the whole night thru. I actually didn't remember much about the letter that I had read. Jerry had briefly mentioned it before he left for work.

He was running a little late for work and didn't help me out of bed. He would have but I told him that Amelia would be there any time and she could help me up. It was only minutes after Jerry went out the door that Amelia had arrived.

I was glad because I really had to use the bathroom. Just as I heard Amelia coming in the front door, I hollered for her to come help me out of bed. I was hollering that I had to pee! She laughed at me. Of course I didn't think it was too funny. I wasn't about to wet the bed.

The day passed by fairly quickly. Jerry came home from work that evening. Little did I know that when I had told him about the vegetables that the Baker family had offered that he would have gone by the old home place to retrieve their offer. He had stopped by there on his way home from work.

Jerry came into the house with his arms loaded down with sacks of the garden goodies. Amelia helped him carry them to the kitchen, and then she left. I called the Baker family and told them how much we appreciated their gift.

Next thing I knew was that Jerry was wheeling me into the kitchen. He was going to cook the fresh foods that the family had given us. I remembered the one time when Jerry had claimed to have cooked us steak and potatoes and when I had found the steakhouse boxes in the trash. I wondered what the food he was about to prepare for us might turn out to be like!

Usually our meals had been prepared by the sitter who stayed with me while Jerry worked. When Jerry was at home and I had no sitter, he usually made us sandwiches or we called for pizza delivery.

A little bit afraid about Jerry's cooking, I attempted to help Jerry with as much of the cooking as I could but it wasn't easy being that I was limited to standing up for very long by myself. Jerry had helped me out of my wheelchair and had placed me into a kitchen chair next to the counter top. My crutches were close by. While I was mostly sitting, I watched as Jerry chopped and battered the fresh garden veggies.

Occasionally, though I struggled, I would pull myself up from the kitchen chair while holding to the kitchen table for support and I would stand with my crutches under my arms and prop myself up over the stove to stir something for him. Jerry attempted to help me up from the kitchen chair but I told him I needed to do it myself. I had to learn to do for myself. He did kind of keep his hands within my reach in case I fell, but I succeeded on my own.

I gave Jerry my input about seasoning the vegetables and of when something was finished cooking. When I gave him any advice about cooking the meal he reassured me that he knew what he was doing.

To my surprise, with my input, Jerry had cooked up a most delicious smelling country supper. The aroma was making my mouth water. He had prepared corn on the cob, golden brown fried squash, fresh mashed potatoes, though they were a bit lumpy, corn bread fritters, fresh green beans and had slices of juicy red tomatoes. All of which had been grown right from the soil of my old home place. It really made me homesick in a way.

As I mostly had watched as Jerry had prepared the foods, my mind temporarily had shifted from the good smelling foods and had went to a place of self pity and self disgust. I began thinking of how I used to raise a garden myself. I thought about how I used to get out there and work in my garden every evening. Sometimes till dark. Now I could barely get myself out the front door without help.

I wanted to just die sometimes when I thought about what I'd lost. I wanted to be able to walk again and use my hands, comb my own hair, plant a garden, do things without the help of others! I was upset that I was limited to what I could do!

Not that I wasn't thankful for what God had given me back! I was just having selfish thoughts! I wanted sight in both my eyes! It just wasn't fair! I knew that I would never regain my eyesight in the right eye. At least that's what the doctor's had said. Not even corrective surgery could repair the damage that had been done to my eyes.

God had given back so much to me. Why was I complaining! Just be grateful Sandy I thought to myself! You have a handsome husband, great friends, and you're alive! You at least can feel again! You can speak! You are learning to walk again! God allowed you to walk, though with crutches, down the isle and marry the man of your dreams. And such a wonderful man too! For that man had been standing over a hot stove in the hot summer time just to cook a meal for you!

My mind started telling me to stop being foolish and to stop feeling sorry for myself and that God loved me!

Quickly my mind then went back to the wonderful smelling country cooking. Jerry had already set the table with plates and had put food in each of them. He slid the kitchen chair that I was now sitting in up to the kitchen table.

Jerry and I together gave thanks to God for the food, our lives and for God's undying love and then we enjoyed every bite of the food that was prepared before us.

Little did I know, but God was still working miracles with my life. As time goes by the miracles of God are shown to many, but our troubles, they haven't even begun yet!

Chapter Seven

WHERE WAS TODD ADAMS

Another year had passed. It had now been four and a half years since the torturous events I had endured. Only by the grace of God, I could now lift myself up from the wheelchair with little struggle. I could get myself up and stand on both feet pretty well with only minimal use of my crutches and the walker. All without the help from anyone.

I was getting my independence back! I had regained most of the feeling and use of my hands. The paralysis that had stricken me was less evident.

Everyone including myself was amazed that I could be up and around for a couple of hours without having to rest.

After Tammy Jackson taking me to the therapist/doctor and being examined, it proved I was doing better than anyone had ever expected. For while I was at the doctor visit, the doctors said it was a miracle that I had gotten this far.

To the doctors' surprise, and only a miracle, I had even regained a little bit of sight in the right eye. The doctor's couldn't explain why. The doctors had all agreed that it was probably just a temporarily thing going on. I did not believe that! I believed that God was healing me. I believed that God was working on the internal scars, as well as the outer scars.

Up until this point of my life I hadn't been able to do much except for what little I attempted to straighten on the house and pray and talk to God. He was the pilot of my life. I owed my life to him. He had saved me from death and he was little by little restoring my life. Completely!

On the eve following that doctor's appointment, Jerry had arrived home from work. I was telling Jerry about the good news from the therapist /doctor visit. Jerry was very happy for me. He too had faith in God that I would soon be totally healed. He knew that God was the miracle worker in my life. He felt as I did about my eyesight. He knew that God could and was correcting that too! With God, I knew that anything was possible.

After talking to Jerry and telling him about my progress, I told him that I was going to go lie down and rest for a while. He was okay with that, but first he said he wanted to discuss something with me. I had no idea of what he wanted to discuss with me.

He and I were sitting side by side on our sofa when I saw Jerry reach into his coat pocket. I knew he wasn't about to pull out an engagement ring for we were already married. I was stunned, totally in shock when I saw what I saw and heard what he had to say!

He proceeded to tell me that he had purchased a hand gun. He pulled the gun from his coat pocket. He wanted me to learn to use it.

I didn't want any part of a gun! I was totally refusing it. I told Jerry that I didn't even like the thought of having a gun in our home. I begged him to please put it away and get it out of our home!

He raised himself from the sofa as he tried to explain his reasons for buying the gun. He was saying that he got the gun for my protection. He was pleading with me to at least think about learning to use it.

He knew that I was furious that he had brought a gun into our home, and still knowing that, he told me that he was putting the gun into my dresser drawer. He was being bull headed and stubborn! He turned away and headed toward our bedroom.

Both of us were being bull headed and stubborn. We didn't have another word to say to each other for the rest of that evening. Matter of fact, when bedtime came, Jerry had slept on the sofa. It was funny in a way because that had been our first and only disagreement since we had been married.

The next morning came. Jerry had gotten up and made coffee. He brought me a cup to my bedside. We talked. After some discussion about the gun, I finally agreed to allow the gun to stay in the house but I still refused to learn to shoot it. Jerry and I patched up our differences.

For a couple of days the gun just lay in my dresser drawer. There was no way that I would ever pick up a gun, much less shoot one!

Then one day while I was all alone in our home I began to think about Amber. I didn't have a need for a caretaker to be with me anymore. I began to think about what might happen if I ever came face to face with Amber again. I would surely be terrified but I couldn't just let Amber hurt me again. I needed some kind of defense!

I thought of everything that I might be able to use to protect myself in the case if something ever did happen. I thought about mace or a kitchen knife! I thought about a baseball bat! I thought about getting a mean dog!

Nothing that I thought about seemed to be as sensible as having a gun and knowing how to use one. Thinking about all this made me go and open the dresser drawer. I thought I could build my courage up about using a gun! It took a few tries for me to even pick up the gun from the drawer but finally I did it.

I would take out the gun and look at it. I was thinking maybe I should try to learn to shoot the thing. Then I'd change my mind and put the gun back. I probably took the gun out of the drawer and put it back in at least four or five times. I went back and forth with this, finally deciding that I needed to learn to use it.

I put the gun back into its resting place. I didn't know if the gun was loaded and was glad that after thinking about it that the gun didn't go off in my hand.

When Jerry came home from work that evening I told Jerry I was ready to learn to shoot the gun. He was pleased with my decision.

That next day Jerry had set up a target in our backyard for me to practice shooting. From that day on, Jerry worked with me every evening for about a month or so teaching me to shoot the gun. I had gotten pretty good, he had told me.

After Jerry feeling confident about me handling the gun, he had made me promise to keep the gun in my possession at all times. It didn't matter if I went outside or was ever alone inside the house, but to take it with me where ever I was.

I did as he ask, though I always felt kind of silly carrying a gun outside in my own yard and into the bathroom of our home. Silly or not, I had made a promise and I was going to keep it!

I continued with my practice a couple times a week. I myself now felt comfortable around guns. I wasn't near as afraid. The gun actually gave me a sense of security.

The days pass as Jerry and I enjoy our married life together. I felt secure and safe. I was at a point in my life that I felt I could handle anything. I was on top of the world!

Then on another afternoon Jerry and I were sitting together on the couch. We were watching the nightly news on TV. An announcer interrupted the regular news broadcast. Across the TV screen flashed "BREAKING NEWS".

The announcer was saying:
We have received information that a body was found near the waters of the Cherokee Lake. The body has been identified as that of Todd Adams. He was the wanted felon for rape and attempted murder of Sandra Tucker, a local woman.

The announcer went on to speak...
He began describing what had taken place nearly five years ago! The announcer then said... we will have more on the story as we... the sound from the TV faded from my ears.

I felt my heart go right to my feet. I was in shock. I was frightened. I couldn't believe what I'd just heard.

Jerry just put his arms around me and was saying it's going to be okay. He said we will call and verify everything. We will make sure if it's all true.

I stopped Jerry as he was speaking. I said "Amber! What about Amber? Do you think she.....

...Jerry said, now Sandy, don't jump to any conclusions. We don't know the details of what has happened. Then Jerry got on the phone. I sat dumbfounded on the sofa.

I heard Jerry asking questions. It seemed like he was on the telephone for a lifetime. Finally, he had hung up the phone.

Jerry began to tell me that the authorities wanted us to come to the police station. He said the authorities had tried to contact us, but each time they had tried to call they had gotten a voice message and couldn't legally leave us any message. They told Jerry that they had to speak to a real person.

They had told Jerry that they had found a sealed envelope. It had been found on the inside of Todd Adams jacket. They had told Jerry that the name on the envelope was addressed to a Sandra Tucker!

My mind went to thinking about all kinds of thoughts! I wondered why if they had called that I never heard the phone ringing. I hadn't left the house lately except for maybe a doctor visit. That had to be the only time they could have called! I thought about where Todd's body had been found. They had found Todd's body next to Cherokee Lake. The lake which was only a quarter mile away from my old home. Why? How did he get there? I was asking Jerry all these questions that he had no answers to?

Jerry said now Sandy; let's leave all this to the authorities to figure out. We will just go to the station and see about this envelope they have!

Jerry and I proceeded to get ready to go to the police station. Still my mind was going crazy with thoughts! Finally dressed and on our way to Tennessee to the station, the drive was long and tiring.

We arrived at the station. The officer that had been on the scene of the crime came over to me. He knew who I was because he was the one that had been on the case of Amber and Todd since day one. He handed me an envelope that had Sandra Tucker written on the front of it.

I looked at the name on it. It wasn't for a Sandra or Sandy Haggard! Somebody didn't know that I was married. I didn't know if the letter was from Todd or if someone had placed it inside his coat.

Then I heard the officer say to me that after I had read what was inside the envelope that he would need it back for evidence.

I ripped opened the envelope and pulled out a folded sheet of paper. I opened the folded paper so that I could see what was written on it. With Jerry at my side, as my hands were shaking and uncontrollable, he helped me with putting on my reading glasses and helped hold the paper.

It read:

Dear Sandy,

I'm writing this note to you to say I'm sorry for what I did to you. I just got caught up with everything with Amber. I'm sorry for raping you. I know you were begging me to stop, but I was so mad at Amber, I couldn't stop. I hope you can forgive me. I told Amber what happened on that day between us. She went off like a lit fire cracker. She has never forgiven me. I guess I can't blame her for that. Amber and I hurt you badly. I let Amber drag me into her situation. She is a crazy psychopath. She has some mental problems. I must admit that I do too! Amber has promised that she will finish you off. She is just waiting for the right time. That's what she told me! I told Amber I wanted out of our relationship. She went crazy. I had to leave her. She said she would get even with me too. Amber told me a story about her mother. She said that her mother had left her alone as a child and she had to kill her mother. She says you left her, so she has to kill you too Sandy. Now that I have left her, I am sure that she will kill me too if she finds me! If I'm found dead, and you find this letter, you'll know Amber had something to do with it, and also know, that she is somewhere very near by just waiting to finish you off. Again Sandy, I'm very sorry, please forgive me and watch your back!!!!

Signed, Todd Adams

Thoughts began to flood my mind as I finished reading the letter from Todd. I did feel sorry for Todd Adams. He was taken in by Amber just as I was. But could I forgive him for what he did to me? He was trying to warn me that Amber hadn't given up on hurting me, killing me. He had left Amber. He had died. Did Amber kill him?

I had so many questions. I was scared for my life, again! I had just begun to feel normal. Was everything starting over? Where was Amber?

Todd Adams had now paid for what he had done to me. He had paid by losing his own life. Now he has to answer to God for the wrongs he had done! I must forgive him, but I will never forget what he did to me.

With all the thoughts going on inside my head, finally, I had made my mind up about something. I turned my attention back to the officer. I gave the torn envelope and letter back to the officer.

As he had reached for the envelope, he asks me did I want to be put in protective custody. Still shaking, I said NO! Though I was terrified, I wasn't going to hide from Amber. That was the something that I had made my mind up about a long time ago!

I began hollering loudly to the officer as if it was his fault about everything that had happened. Everyone inside the police station was stunned at my outwardly reaction! Jerry too! Nobody was saying a word as I let off steam about how I felt!

I was screaming at the officer that if Amber wanted me, she would try to get me no matter where I was! I screamed that Amber could have probably already gotten me if she had of wanted to. I screamed for them to read the letter! Todd says she has been near me all the while! Amber has promised she will get me!

As I was hatefully thrashing my feelings out to the officer my words finally began to calm. I began saying to the officer in a more reasonable voice that I had Jerry to protect me. I had God to protect me! They would be at my side.

I told the officer that I had my phone. I promised that if anything seemed out of the ordinary, I would call 911.

I then looked toward Jerry so that the officer couldn't hear what I was going to say and I told Jerry that I have my hand gun and thanked him for teaching me to shoot it. I just hoped I would never have to use it!

Then turning back toward the officer, I promised him and Jerry that I wouldn't answer our door at home if anyone should come unannounced or if I didn't know who was on the other side of it. I promised myself that I wouldn't let Amber hurt me ever again. I had God on my side!!!

After the officer was done with me, Jerry drove us back to our home. With Jerry's help, I went into the house. I wanted to soak in the tub. I ran myself a tub of hot water and stepped into it.

While soaking in the tub of water my mind began wandering again. At first I thought of how the hot water felt so good on my skin. That reminded me of the scars I still have from the burns I had received from where Amber and Todd had put me in a tub of acidy water.

I wondered how anyone could be that cruel! The acid that had been added to the bath water was an acid used to clean electronic parts. Todd had worked at such a place. There had been just enough acid added to the water to severely burn the skin and cause me to be scarred for the rest of my life.

I began to wonder why and how had Todd let Amber get him involved in her craziness? I wondered how anyone could be that stupid!

But then I thought about how easy it was for me to feel sorry for Amber. Amber had a way about her that you would have trusted her with your life. I guess Todd trusted Amber with his life a little bit to long. Look what happened to him! I trusted Amber with my life too. Look what happen to me!

I began to think about how I was still in danger until Amber was captured or dead. I guess I was stupid too. But I wouldn't be stupid again!

Then my mind went back to when Jerry and I were at the police station. I recalled the officer's words as he had described the scene where Todd Adams dead body had been found. My body shivered as I pictured the scene in my mind!

The officer had said that Todd had been beaten with a large object. It appeared to have been several blows to the head that had actually killed him. Todd's private parts had been cut off. He had been stabbed in the neck and the chest with a knife. His throat had been slashed. His tortured body had probably been slain for several days. It was believed that all of this had taken place right at the lake where his slain body was found.

I recalled the officer saying that a young man had found the body and had called 911. I found out later that the young man that had made the 911 call was the son of the new owners of my old home place.

The new owners' son whom was now only about sixteen, had been out hiking on the land and had gotten lost. To think that Todd would have never been found if this young man hadn't gotten lost. If they hadn't bought that property, Todd would probably have just rotted out there.

Then I thought about how the buzzards would have probably ate Todd's decomposed body. What a scary thought! To never be found and to be eaten by buzzards!!! Oh my God, that could have been me! Amber could have killed me and left me for the birds to devour my body!

My thoughts then turned to the bath water that I had been soaking in. It had cooled. Though it felt good on my scarred skin, I needed to get out of the tub and get myself ready for bed. I was worn out! I finished my bath and went into my bedroom. After dressing myself for bed, I knelt down to my knees at my bedside. I begin to pray to God. I ask God to watch over me and to be my shield of armor. I didn't want to end up like Todd. I prayed for God to protect Jerry and my friends. I didn't know what Amber might try to do, if anything, to them! I prayed for God to make the days ahead bearable and gave God the thanks for what he had already done in my life.

Chapter Eight

THE FUNERAL

Todd Adams was laid to rest. There were many plain clothed security officers all around. The officers thought that Amber might try to come around. They sure didn't want to take any chances of that happening. They thought she might try to disguise herself as someone else. They kept a watchful eye out for her appearance. They promised me that if she did show up, she wouldn't get away this time.

I was terrified that Amber would show herself but I wasn't going to let her run my life. If she came to kill me and succeeded then so be it! Either way, I wasn't running from her any more! I didn't think Amber cared if she got caught as long as she got to finish what she started. I believed she'd take that chance.

Todd Adams wasn't from Tennessee. He was from Utah. I thought it was a bit strange that none of his family had shown up for his funeral. None of Todd's family would bury him either. The state of Tennessee had to foot the bill. The state would have to bury him here. The cost to ship his remains to Utah would be costly, and his family didn't want to claim Todd anyway.

However, one of his family members, an anonymous sister, did send a letter to the funeral home in care of me. I wondered how a sister of Todd's knew about me. I would find that out in the letter. When the letter was brought to me I opened it and begin to read it.

Todd's sister had apologized for what Todd had done to me. She said Todd had a mental past. She said that all of his family had disowned him years ago. She said Todd had abused many of his family members and friends.

She wrote that her brother was at one time in a mental hospital. His sister had said in her letter that the last she had heard from Todd was that he was still in the mental ward. Except for when she saw the news on TV where he was wanted for the rape and attempted murder charges. Then she wrote that he'd showed up in Utah with some woman wanting his family to forgive and forget everything he'd done to them.

She wrote in her letter that when Todd realized that he wasn't wanted in Utah by any of his relatives and that he'd been turned in to the police, he and the woman had left Utah and he hadn't been heard from since!

She wrote that it didn't surprise her at all of what Todd had done. She told in the letter that she had tried to get Todd to turn himself in while he was in Utah but he refused to do so. She wrote and told that she was the one that had called the police when Todd showed up in Utah. Her efforts had been useless, for by the time the police had arrived to capture Todd, he had already fled.

The sister wrote that she loved her brother Todd and had forgiven him for the things he had done in his life. She asks me to forgive her brother for what he had done to me. There was no return address on the letter or envelope nor was there a name for his sister.

Todd's funeral was short and a quick one. There were very few people that attended the service considering nobody claimed Todd. Sad but true, the attendants were only Jerry and myself, my friend Amelia and the girls from the salon along with a handful of co-workers that had worked with Todd at the factory where he had stolen the acid that had burned me. Then there were the plain clothed policemen!

It was a closed casket service for Todd. His body was too mutilated for an open casket. A few of Todd's co-workers had stood up in front of the congregation and said a nice thing or two about Todd. I wondered if what they had said about Todd was real. The co-workers stated that Todd had been a dedicated worker and a pleasant person to talk to. I never knew the Todd that they spoke of. As for me, I didn't speak a word on behalf of Todd. I didn't have a good thing to say about him, so I chose to keep quiet.

Thankfully, Amber never appeared at the funeral. Nobody saw her there. It's strange but I felt sure that she was somewhere near. It was just one of those feelings you get!

The funeral home had cleared very quickly after the service for Todd. Jerry took me home right after. It wasn't nowhere near our bedtime but all I wanted to do was go to sleep. I hoped it would take my mind off everything that had happened. I fell asleep as quickly as my head had hit my pillow.

After a short but peaceful sleep, luckily, without any bad dreams, Jerry had awakened me. I felt rested but as soon as my eyes opened, the horrible thoughts about Todd and Amber were back on my mind.

Jerry wanted me to get up. He said he was taking me out for supper. Jerry thought that food and going out would take both our minds off of what we had been through.

I told Jerry that I thought it was too late to go out! I said to him, "goodness, we haven't been out in forever" and I sort of laughed about it!

He wasn't giving up. He said to me "come on Sandy, we can call it a date"! He sort of laughed as in a way that said that we were too old for dating! It had been years since we had actually been out on a date together! It had been years since we had been out late at night!

Being that Jerry laughed and was making me feel old, I decided that I was hungry! Besides, I knew that he wouldn't quit trying to get me to go out. He was as stubborn as I was. Somebody had to give in!

I got up from my bed and slipped my shoes on and we left the house for what would be a well deserved and needed date.

To my surprise, Jerry was taking me to the small cafe called the Red Barn not far from our house here in Trina Alabama. It had been a favorite place of ours. We had had our first real date there years ago. Jerry thought that being at the Red Barn cafe, rekindling some old memories would help to take my mind off everything.

After arriving at the cafe and being seated, a waitress came to take our food order. As we had always ordered way back when, we had burgers and fries. The food hadn't changed that much. It was still just as good as I had remembered!

Jerry and I talked and reminisced about old times as we sat and ate our burgers and fries. We held hands like we were high school sweethearts. I talked about how good it felt to be able to go out in public and not be in a wheel chair. It was a good feeling to go out and feel a bit of freedom. I told Jerry of how I was uncomfortable about the people who were staring at me. I knew they were staring at my scarred face.

He assured me that I was beautiful. He said that some people are just ignorant and ill mannered.

Jerry nor I spoke a word about Todd or Amber while at the cafe. I was glad that neither of them had barely crossed my mind. Even so, I still felt the need to look over my shoulder. Especially after just burying

Amber's boyfriend and knowing what Todd had written in his letter.

After finishing our food and having a few cups of coffee over conversation, I was tired. I was talked out! I ask Jerry to take me home. Being a gentleman, Jerry helped me from my seat and escorted me to the car.

The ride home was quiet. Maybe too quiet! For once again, my mind was spinning with all the thoughts from the past of Amber, the letter found on Todd Adams body and the letter from Todd's no name sister.

I guess Jerry was reading my mind. He reached over with his hand and took my hand as he steered the car with his other. He asks was I okay?

The touch of Jerry's hand on mine and the love and concern I had heard in his words as he asks if I was okay really broke me down. I was very lucky to have such a wonderful and caring man.

Suddenly I felt my heart wanting to break inside. I couldn't answer Jerry's question. I was so choked up that I couldn't speak, but I knew that Jerry could hear my sniffles as I was trying so hard to fight back my tears. I didn't want to cry. I didn't want to be weak. I didn't want Jerry to see me falling apart again, as he'd seen so many times over the past years. I didn't want to spoil the evening we had just shared!

I had so many different emotions going on inside my body all at the same time but couldn't explain them! I was sad but I was happy. I was thankful but at times I was ungrateful. I was afraid but courageous. I was numb. I was an emotional wreck!

Why did I have to be like this! It seemed that every time I would get to a place in my life where I was coping with the past and forgetting, something would happen to rekindle those terrible memories.

With me still sniffling and trying so hard not to cry, Jerry pulled the car off to the side of the road and stopped. He turned to me and put his arms around me to hold and comfort me. That's when my tears came like rain. It was no holding them back. I didn't know what I would do if I didn't have Jerry at times like that. He held me until I had cried myself out.

After being comforted by my husband, my tears had finally subsided so we took back to the road. I must have been more tired than I had realized. I had fallen asleep during our travel. I was awakened by Jerry when we arrived at home.

With Jerry and I now inside our home, I was in my comfort zone. I felt safest behind our closed and locked doors. Curtains drawn shut! Windows nailed down!

All I wanted to do was go lie down and go back to sleep. Jerry and I got ready for bed. While he and I lay together, his hand stroked my brow and my hair. That was his way to let me know he was there for me and that everything would be okay. At some point I fell asleep.

The next morning when I woke up, I looked at the clock hanging on our bedroom wall. It was 9:15 am. I didn't see Jerry anywhere. I called out his name and he didn't answer. I wasn't frightened of being alone because Jerry had on many occasions gotten up before I did. And as I had said before, I was in my comfort zone.

I figured that Jerry had gotten up and left for work. A note on the bedside table confirmed what I had thought. The note read as follows: "Didn't want to wake you after last night. Call me if you need me and remember that I love you and have a wonderful day. Otherwise, I'll see you tonight". Love Jerry

Being that I was now capable of getting myself up without the help of others and I didn't need a sitter anymore, Jerry knew that I would be fine. My walker was my sitter! Things were still a little difficult to do by myself sometimes but I was determined to do for myself.

Feeling the need to pray, I got up out of bed and knelt down on my knees and began to pray to God. After prayer and Jerry's note I felt so much better. It was moments like this that made me feel strong. Prayer seemed to take the weight of the world off my shoulders. At least for a time being.

Though I didn't need a sitter anymore, Tammy would still come to my house to check on me from time to time. As usual, Tammy and I did a lot of talking whenever she came. Not necessarily on any particular subject.

I guess I had been up out of bed for about an hour when I heard a knock on the door. At first I felt a little frightened. Then I heard someone call out my name. It was Tammy. She had forgotten her key to our house.

I wasn't expecting her but was glad that she came to visit. On this day that Tammy came, like any other, she and I were talking about things regarding the salon or her son. Then during our conversation Tammy had changed the subject to Todd Adams and Amber Lynn Newby. The things that she told me sent chills over my body! What she would eventually find out would shock everyone. There was more to Amber than anyone would ever imagine!

Chapter Nine

TAMMY

Soon after Todd Adams death and he had been laid to rest things began to surface about Amber Lynn Newby. I knew that Tammy had been trying to find out about Amber's background but what I didn't know was that Tammy was closer than she herself had even realized of finding horrible tragedies regarding Amber.

It all started with the anonymous letter from Todd's sister. The day that Tammy had came to my house and we conversed about Todd and Amber, Tammy had told me of a horrible happening she had learned about. Her findings terrified me!

Right after Todd's funeral, Tammy had begun a search on Todd and had possibly found a couple of his family members. After some digging into Todd's past,

Tammy came across a phone number of the "could be" relative of Todd's. Tammy told me that she called the number and indeed it was a relative of Todd's.

After her telephone conversation with Todd's family member, which was a male cousin of Todd's, Tammy was told that Todd and Amber had been in Utah! The cousin confirmed that Amber was the woman that Todd had taken to Utah with him to attempt to reconnect with his family.

Todd's cousin had told Tammy, that during a conversation he had had with Todd, he found out that Amber was from Georgia. That information led Tammy to some major sickening information regarding Amber. Tammy's findings were very frightening.

As Tammy told me about the things she had found on Amber my stomach got weak. I thought I was going to throw up. I wasn't really sure that I wanted to hear what Tammy was telling me.

Tammy had found out that Amber did in fact kill her mother. She had found out about the happening in an archive of an old Georgia news paper. It dated back nearly twenty years ago.

Though Tammy had a copy of the old article in her hand, a picture of a young Amber plastered just above the writing, as I listened to Tammy read the article to me I wondered if maybe she had did a search on someone else. Though this article Tammy was reading sounded so familiar to what I had been thru myself, I wondered if maybe there had been another person with the name of Amber Lynn Newby. I could barely believe my ears but it was all so true.

The old news article was written as follows:

Fifteen Year Old Amber Lynn Newby
<u>Was It Self Defense</u>

The investigation that had been going on regarding the abuse of the adolescent girl Amber Lynn Newby has now been halted. Tragic as it seems, the suspected abusers have been found dead. It appears that the cause of death of the mother is from being stabbed multiple times in the back and also in her head. The step father died from a gun shot to the chest.

The fifteen year old girl, Amber, has not been found at this time. It is now known that the daughter, Amber Lynn Newby is the person that has done this terrible act to her mother and step father.

There is physical evidence that links Amber to the crime. Some may call it self defense! I call it plain out right **murder**!

As some of you may know, the state had been investigating the girls' parents for a long while now. For those of you that don't recall what had been going on then let me refresh your memory.

It all began when Amber Lynn Newby's school teacher had made the claim to the school board that she saw bruises on Amber. It was believed that Amber was being beaten by her mother and step father. The stepfather had allegedly raped Amber. Amber had told her teacher many things that were being done to her.

The teacher told the school board that Amber had not been showing up for school. The reason Amber had given to her teacher for missing school so much was that her mother locked her in a closet for days and nearly starved her and beat her to death. The teacher told that Amber had stated that while being locked away in a closet, that the mother only fed Amber a few crackers a day and that she barely survived. As thin as Amber seemed to be, the teacher thought that Amber could be speaking truths.

The teacher also stated that Amber seemed to be a troubled child. The teacher told authorities that Amber didn't make friends very well. She told that Amber was a lonely girl. Amber seemed to be a severely deeply depressed young girl.

The school teacher had put the authorities onto Amber's mother and stepfather regarding suspected abuse, but sadly things have turned from bad to worse.

As to the whereabouts of Amber Lynn Newby, at this time, nobody knows where she is. Amber is now fifteen years old. If she is captured she may have to stand trial as an adult. The question has been asked if Amber was dangerous to others? The officials seem to think that Amber has no reason to want to harm another. They only ask should anyone see Amber or know her whereabouts, please contact the Georgia Police Department.

Was it Self defense! I think not!

The news paper then gives a telephone number to call if Amber is sighted. The writer's name of the article then appears at the end.

After Tammy had done a bit more of investigating, she found that the Georgia law officials had let the case go cold. The Georgia investigators didn't have a clue as to where Amber had run off to. And for the nearly twenty years past that Amber had been running from the law they didn't know it but Amber had been living right up under their noses.

After all Amber had come from Kentucky when she began working for me at the salon. She lived in Tennessee for many months while working at the salon. She had been in Alabama. Georgia was only hours away!

I still get the shivers when I think about what Tammy had found on Amber. I wondered how Amber had steered clear of the law all these years! I guessed the same way she had for the past years since she had nearly killed me!

As for the article stating that no one considered Amber dangerous to another, they were so very wrong! I wondered why nobody in the Georgia law enforcement had not connected with the law enforcement over in Tennessee. They had to have heard about what Amber had done to me at my Tennessee home.

If the information about Amber killing her mother and stepfather had surfaced in our area or news media before now, maybe none of the horrible things that had happened to me, and even Todd, would have ever happened in the first place.

It would be found out later that in the years that had past, somehow, with changes within the Georgia police department, all the critical information about Amber, that had thought to have been stored away for safe keeping had been destroyed or stolen. No records were on file. It was as if the killings never happened. If it hadn't been for the old news paper article that Tammy had come across, Amber basically had gotten away with murdering her family!

As it stands at this time, Amber will have three murder charges against her and one attempted murder charge and a string of other offenses to be tried for. That is, if she is ever captured.

Now with this new information, to make things worse, Tammy was missing! I know it has something to do with Amber. I think that maybe Amber realized that Tammy was on to her! Tammy would not just disappear!

I realized that Tammy had gone missing after Tammy had called me on the phone. During a quick conversation, Tammy seeming excited told me that she was coming over to my house. She had something to tell me she had said! Tammy sounded anxious and a little bit nervous on the phone. Tammy didn't want to discuss what she wanted to tell me about over the phone! She stated to me that she was on her way and for me to keep my doors locked.

I begged Tammy to tell me what the call was all about but in her excited anxious way, she had hung up the phone before I could get anything out of her. I had waited for Tammy to arrive and when she didn't show up I tried to call her back. I didn't get an answer. I called Tammy's phone repeatedly and still got no answer. I began to worry! I called everyone that knew Tammy. Nobody had heard from her! Nobody could reach her by phone!

By this time Jerry was at home from work. I told Jerry about Tammy calling and saying she was on her way to our house and that she had something to tell me. I told him about Tammy wanting me to keep my doors locked. That frightened the both of us. Not really knowing what to do, Jerry and I called the police and told them about Tammy calling me. We told the police of what Tammy had said over the phone which wasn't much. It wasn't long that a policeman had arrived at our home.

We didn't know if Tammy was wanting to warn us that Amber was about to strike or what. The officer did a search over our property and surrounding areas. Nothing seemed suspicious or out of the ordinary.

While the officer was at our home, we discussed Tammy's disappearance. The officer explained to us that a person had to be missing for so many hours before they could officially declare them a missing person. The policeman leaves.

The time passes. Still no word from Tammy! Where was she! What did she need to tell me! Twenty four hours later, finally the search was on for Tammy!

The days became weeks and still Tammy was nowhere to be found!

Then a month had passed since Tammy had been reported missing and luckily but sad, her car was found. It was found in the Tennessee River. A passerby had spotted it. The passerby had noticed something shiny in the waters of the river. At first the passerby had did just that. They had went on past but something told them to turn around and go back to see what the shiny object might be.

Thankfully, the passerby had turned around. As they had gotten out of their vehicle and walked down closer to where the shiny object had been seen, they realized that it was actually a red taillight of a car. The river water was low because of lack of rain and the flow of the water had pushed the car just in the right place for a taillight to show.

The passerby contacted the police. The police arrived with a towing truck and divers and the likes. The vehicle was pulled from the river. The police confirmed that the car belonged to Tammy. It appeared to be an accident.

Tammy's purse and cell phone was found in the car. Everything inside her purse was soaked with water. That wasn't good! It was a hope that there might be something inside the purse to lead investigators to figure out what Tammy desperately wanted to tell me. No such luck. All of the contents in the purse were ruined! One of Tammy's shoes was found. Tammy wasn't in the car!

The search and rescue team searched for Tammy in the river and surrounding areas for several weeks, but she was never found!

As time went by, Tammy was officially pronounced dead! Tammy's family gave her a proper burial and was trying to go on with their life. I couldn't and didn't want to believe that Tammy was gone.

Tammy's mother and father were now taking care of Tammy's son. I go and visit them from time to time. It was heartbreaking for me to see Tammy's son and to see how much he had grown. When I look into those little boys eyes I see his mother. The little fellow was now seven years old. Though my heart broke for the child, I was glad that he had his mother's honest, caring, loving, and yes sometimes her hot headed ways!

It was hard for me not to blame myself for that little boy's loss. Knowing that Tammy was headed to my house the day her car went off into the Tennessee River. I knew that Tammy was most likely going to tell me something else she may have found out about Amber! If only I'd not gotten mixed up with Amber, then this little boy would still have his mom!

Sadly, the horror stories weren't over for any of us yet.

Chapter Ten

TO LIVE OR DIE

As the next few months passed I was able to do most anything I wanted to do. I didn't need the crutches anymore. The wheelchair was a thing of the past! It was actually collecting dust! I could get up and down and walk just as well as anyone could! Well almost! I still had this little limp!

Only by the grace of God, my body and my eyesight was good enough that I was able to get in my car and drive myself to where I wanted to go. I carried my walker with me just in case I needed that extra help but most times I made it fine without it. I felt like I was no longer a burden on anyone.

My gun hand was perfect. Except for the shake I sometimes have caused from nerve damage. I was in the ninety nine percent range of recovery. The doctor's tell me that I'm a walking miracle! I know that God did it all! The doctor's laugh when I tell them that nobody's perfect and that I could live with the one percent imperfection!

I was at a point in my life that Amber rarely crossed my mind. Whenever I did have a thought of that time, I knew I was stronger. I was able to brush the thoughts aside and go on with my life.

It would soon be five years since the attack. The anniversaries of the attack and my birthdays had always been the roughest. Somehow, I knew or at least I hoped and prayed that this anniversary/birthday would be different. I had a new outlook on life. I give God all the credit, for God had helped me, guided me and gave me the strength to keep looking ahead and not giving up.

My birthday was just a week away. I was at home when I heard my cell phone ringing. I went and picked it up. I saw the caller ID. It was Jerry calling me from work. I answered it! I said hi babe! What's up?

His response was that he wanted me to get ready to go out. He would be home to pick me up in about an hour, he said. We would go to our favorite place. The Red Barn Cafe.

The Red Barn Cafe wasn't fancy or nothing, just an old cafe with an old fashioned Jukebox that played old timey music and the burgers were hand pattied and greasy but delicious.

Jerry and I exchanged I love you's over the phone then I told Jerry I'd be ready to go when he got home. I hung up the phone.

I went to the bathroom and got a quick shower and then dressed for the occasion. Blue jeans and a flannel button down shirt with a pair of old tennis shoes will do just fine. I brushed my teeth. Then with a little make-up to the face to cover my scars as best I could and towel dried hair, I was ready to go.

Before I knew it, Jerry was home. He quickly changed into his jeans and boots, combed and sprayed his hair then brushed his teeth. He was ready to go.

We got into his car and headed for the cafe. Finally arriving and inside and to my surprise, the girls from the salon were all there, except of course, Tammy. The salon was still up and running. Tammy's parents had taken over the responsibility of running the place. That was good. All of the girls got to keep their job.

After hugging all of the girls and everyone making a fuss over me of how well I was doing and telling me I looked like my old self, we picked out a private area to sit together. We didn't want our noise we would be making to disturb other customers. We had to put a couple of tables together to have enough room for everyone.

The waitress came for our order. Some were undecided about what they wanted, so everyone ordered soda or coffee. The waitress would come back for our food order later. All of us were rattling to each other and sipping on our drink.

A few minutes later the waitress came back and had taken our food orders. After ordering and waiting on our food, Jerry spoke up and said, now I know that ya'll are wondering why I got you all together here tonight. Everyone was like yeah, why?

He said, you all know Sandy has been through a lot over the past years. Her birthday will be next week. You all know she hasn't gotten to celebrate her birthday since the assault on her. Matter of fact, he said to them, Sandy hasn't got to do much of anything with her friends since the incident!

Everyone was quiet while Jerry was making his speech. He went on talking. He said, what I'd like to do for Sandy is to invite you all back here at the Red Barn Cafe for a birthday party. She has come a long way. We would not only be celebrating her birthday but also her recovery. Every ear was tuned in to Jerry. He went on to tell the girls that the doc's had released me from their care. He told them that I no longer had to go to therapy.... and he continued to explain.

After Jerry shut up, everyone agreed it would be a great celebration and all would be there.

The evening went on for hours. The jukebox was playing all the oldies. A customer continued to put quarters in, so we got free music. We all laughed and were having a good time. Before I knew it, it was down to just Jerry and myself. Everyone else has left.

Jerry asks me to dance. It would be the first time I'd danced in years except for when we danced arm and chair back at home. I was a little bit afraid to try to dance but Jerry promised not to let me fall.

With the music flowing from the jukebox, Jerry and I made our way to the center of the cafe floor. A few customers were still hanging around and having coffee. As Jerry placed his arms around me and I the same, our bodies seemed to become one. I felt like my old self again. I loved Jerry more than ever right at this time. He was so good to me and for me.

The song ended. Jerry escorted me back to my seat. Just as we started off the cafe "dance floor", the customers gave us a loud round of applause. Their faces showed that they knew who I was and that they were proud that I had recovered.

Time passes and eventually the cafe was empty except for Jerry and me. The cafe workers had already shut down the grills and had cleaned the place for closing except for our table. The manager had to come and tell us it was time to go. We actually walked out of the cafe with the manager as he was locking up.

The next week seemed to fly by. It was Friday. February 25th, my birthday. Jerry had taken the day off work. He woke me up with a red rose, a cup of coffee and my favorite snack, powdered donuts, all placed neatly on a breakfast tray. He kissed me and said Happy Birthday.

As I sipped at my coffee, Jerry told me that he had the whole day planned out for my birthday. He started telling me of the plans. He said first thing was to get up out of bed and get ready for an outdoor adventure!

He told me that we would take a drive into the mountains and look at the wild out doors. While there up in the mountains, we would stop for lunch. There was a camp sight and park area on the mountain side for visitors to enjoy. We would pack a picnic lunch. He would then take me to the library to get me a new book to read. He knew how I loved to read. Especially since I had gotten my eye sight given back to me. Then we would come back to the house and take a rest before getting ready to go to the Red Barn cafe for my birthday party.

When he finished telling me of his plans for us for the day, I remarked to him that it was going to be a perfect birthday.

I set up in bed. I was so thankful for the things I could do again! I sipped my coffee and ate a couple of donuts holding them with my own two hands!

Jerry had brought his cup of coffee in with him. He had set it on the bedside table on his side of the bed. He sat on the bed beside me and we shared coffee and talked for awhile longer. Finally, Jerry said, if we are going to get this day going, we'd better get up and get ready for it!

I went to the bathroom and got into the shower. Jerry had followed me. We ended up back in the bed and made passionate love to each other. Our love making was sensuous and afterwards, I told Jerry that he had started the day off great as I headed back to the shower again. I joked at him that he hadn't mentioned our love making in the days planning!

With both of us now dressed for the outing, we headed out onto the roads. Up our city street we went and took toward the mountains. The drive in the mountain country was just beautiful. The leaves on the trees were in bloom. Colorful flowers were popped up all over the mountainous roadsides. Spring had arrived early.

I thought about how I used to take things for granted, but after everything I'd been through over the past five years, I looked at things very differently.

We drove along the roads of the mountains and on occasion we would stop and get out of the car to stretch our legs or take a short walk on into the forest like wilderness to catch a glimpse of a baby squirrel or a wild rabbit.

I was beginning to get hungry. I ask Jerry if he was hungry and he was. We turned the car around and headed toward the camp/park grounds.

We finally arrived at the park. It was past lunch time. After looking over the park, we found a little spot under a tree for our picnic. We sat on a blanket and gazed at the sky and watched the clouds and the birds. We shared finger sandwiches and chips. We sipped on ice cold drinks. We watched little children as they played on the swings and slide.

Seeing the little children play made me want a child of my own. But that was one miracle that would never happen. It would never be in the cards. With everything that I had been through, I ended up having to have a complete hysterectomy. My ovaries had been damaged from the hard kicks I had received from Amber. At my age now, I was too old to have a child anyway. I was content with the way things were.

Jerry and I snuggled up to each other on the blanket as we listened to the laughter of the children and the singing of the birds. It was so peaceful here.

The time was passing. I was wishing that we didn't have to leave the park, but we did. We had other things to do. We loaded the car up with our picnic leftovers and headed back into our little city of Trina Alabama.

Next stop was at the public library. I quickly checked out a couple of books that I had been wanting to read and then we drove back to the house. We got the car unloaded and went inside for a short nap.

We slept for about an hour. I woke up before Jerry did. I went and freshened up, and then I woke Jerry. He then went and got himself dressed to leave. It was time to hit the road again. We were to meet everyone at the cafe at 7:00 pm. We headed out the door around 5:00 pm.

As we were going down the interstate, we were about two miles from the exit we needed to take to get us to the Red Barn Cafe. We had been driving for about an hour and forty five minutes. The car started stalling. Jerry eased the car to the right side of the road and the car just died.

Jerry tried to start the car. Nothing happened! It wouldn't start! He looked under the hood. He didn't see anything wrong. He tried to start it again. Still dead! He had always been able to find and fix trouble in our cars before! Why couldn't he fix it now? It must be something pretty major Jerry said! We weren't going anywhere!

We were going to be late for the birthday party. Jerry tried his cell phone to call for help. No service kept coming over his screen. I tried mine. I got the same. No service.

After no success with getting the car going and the cell phones not working and nobody stopping to offer help, Jerry said he would have to walk for help.

There was no way I could go with him. Even though I had recovered remarkably well, I wasn't up to a two-mile walk. Jerry would have to leave me with the car.

I watched him as he walked away from the car. I could see he was still trying his cell phone along the way and then he faded out of sight. I locked the doors on the car. I didn't like being on this big ole highway all alone.

It was around 6:45pm. It was beginning to get dusky dark. Jerry would be back soon! I tried not to think about how long he had been gone! In the meantime, I kept trying my cell phone too. Still no service. What seemed like hours, but was only twenty minutes had passed. It was now 7:05pm.

We should be at the cafe now! I wondered if anyone had realized we weren't there! I then saw lights from a car pull up behind our car. It couldn't be Jerry! He hadn't been gone that long and he would have come from the other side of the interstate.

I had saw several cars pass by and not the first one had offered to stop to see if anyone needed help. Maybe someone was finally going to help. It had gotten darker outside since Jerry had taken off for help. I was a little bit scared!

I couldn't see who was in the car behind ours. I saw the driver's side door of the car open. At first nobody was getting out. Then after a minute or two I saw someone stepping from the car. I couldn't tell if it was a man or woman. I thought maybe a man. The person was approaching the passenger side of our car where I was setting. I had been watching through the mirror on the sun visor. The person had on a ball cap. I thought again, it must be a man.

As the person came closer to our car, I saw that the person had brown hair, which was hanging from beneath the cap. The person seemed tall which made me think that it was a male figure.

I then saw the eyes of the person as the person was getting even closer to my side of the car. The color green. I shivered. Oh my God! It was Amber! I knew those eyes anywhere!

I struggled for my cell phone. I hoped it would work. I tried it! Still no service! All of a sudden, Amber clenched her hands up to the car window and put her face up to it as she looked into the passenger side where I was sitting. I clung to the driver's side of the car as far as I could go. I was scared to death!

Thoughts started flooding my mind. It was happening all over again. I started seeing visions of the past. I kept thinking of what was about to happen. I was praying for God to help me! Why! I had finally made it back to where I used to be! Why now? Why on my birthday? What had I done to deserve this?

I thought, hoped that maybe someone from another passing car would see something going on and stop to help! Nobody was stopping!

Amber begins to strike at the windows of the car with her hands after she realized that the car doors were locked! I saw Amber reach behind her back. She was bringing out a gun. She raised it toward the car window. She tried to fire the gun. It wouldn't shoot! She kept pulling the trigger! It still didn't fire!

She threw the gun across the road, nearly striking a vehicle passing by. The passing vehicle kept going.

I saw Amber running back to the car she had gotten out of. I hoped that she had gotten scared off from the passing car. That wasn't the case. I watched as she opened the trunk and pulled out a tire tool. She was coming back to my car.

My first thought was to get out and run, but I couldn't take that chance. I had nowhere to run to and even though I had recovered tremendously I wasn't able to run anyway! At that moment I didn't think about my gun.

Amber was now back at my car and she had started hammering at the back glass windows with the tire tool! I saw the back glass shatter. Amber was climbing in thru the back.

Oh my God, she was getting in the car! She was kicking some of the glass out of her way. She was so determined! She tried to reach for me.

By this time, I was crumpled into the driver side seat nearly in the floorboard. I was trying to keep away from her. She had gotten nearly into the back seat of the car when her pants had somehow gotten caught by the window frame. She was trying to pull loose from it!

Without thinking, I reached and unlocked the driver side door and flung it open. I had fallen halfway out the door onto my back. Struggling to get up, I then thought about my gun. It was in my purse, which was still in the car.

I could see that Amber was still trying to pull herself loose from the window frame where her pants had gotten hung. I reached into the car for my purse. As I grabbed it, the strap got caught on the gear shift. Amber saw me grabbing at the purse and tried to reach at me again.

I was pulling with everything I had in me. The purse strap broke. The purse and I went flying backwards out the door again. I landed out into the middle of the interstate highway.

By this time Amber had gotten her pants free and was coming out the driver's side door after me. I was trying to stand up and reach into the purse for my gun. I felt the gun and pulled it out. I dropped the purse.

Grasping the gun with both hands, I took aim! I was now standing face to face with Amber just seconds before she could reach me. She had gotten so close that I felt the tips of her finger nails scrap my hand as I had stood up.

When Amber realized I had a gun in her face, she stopped dead still then took a step backwards! I was daring her to move. My hands were shaking as I held my finger on the gun trigger! Just blink an eye, I told her! I would pull the trigger!

Then with one hand holding the gun on Amber and ready to shoot her if I had to, I reached with the other hand and got my cell phone from the holder that was clipped onto my belt. I was praying it would work even though it had not worked up to this point.

I dialed 911. No service! I tried again and again! I was moving the phone around in hopes to find a signal! My gun still in Amber's face! Suddenly, praise God, finally the cell phone was working! Though it was breaking up badly! It was a miracle! God was here! He did that!

I heard a voice say 911 what's your emergency? I proceeded to tell the 911 operator what was happening and where I was. I didn't know if the operator heard what I was telling her or not!

Then I heard the operator say in parts as her voice was breaking up on my end - xxxhelpxxxdispatchxxxstayxxx. The best I could tell was that the operator was dispatching someone as we spoke and she wanted me to stay on the line. Again, whether or not she heard me, I told her I had my hands full and to just get some help here! I hung up the cell phone.

Still holding Amber at gun point, I dialed Jerry's cell phone. It worked again! I was telling him what was going on and told him I loved him. He said he loved me! I was shouting at Amber not to move!

I didn't know if this would be the last time I heard Jerry's voice. Again, I said I love you! I told him help was supposed to be on the way and I didn't know if help would get here in time. I didn't know if Jerry could understand what I'd said. The cell phone was losing connection! Then it went dead! I dropped the phone to the ground.

Amber started trying to get me to put the gun down. I told her the cops were on the way and that no matter what, I would not give in to her sorrowful words this time. I told her I didn't know if I would let her live to see the cops or not.

My mind kept saying pull the trigger. I could call it self-defense! My heart kept saying if you pull that trigger God will not forgive you.

Amber was still begging me not to kill her. With my head spinning, finally I made Amber sit down on the side of the interstate road. My gun still aimed at her head. It was at this time that Amber made the statement to me that she wished I had died in the car accident!

I said; what are you talking about! I was confused! She proceeded to tell me that she was the driver of the other vehicle that night when I had been run off the road! She was saying to me; why didn't you just die! Why didn't you die!

Oh my God, Amber had tried to kill me back then! I had been in a car accident back when Amber had been working for me at the salon. She would have hit me head on if I hadn't jerked my steering wheel to miss her! She apparently didn't care if she would have died that night!

I kept thinking of everything that Amber had put me through. I could pull the trigger! If I didn't kill her, she would possibly go thru what I had gone thru. The last five years of my life had been a living hell! The scars, I'd carry for the rest of my life! Do I let her live or do I just pull the trigger! Where were the cops?

Then my thoughts faded as I saw blue flashing lights approaching. The cop cars quickly halted and out came cops with guns all around us. An officer called out for me to put the gun down. The officer didn't know who was who here.

I yelled out and told him who I was and that I couldn't put the gun down. I said for them to look in the purse laying there on the road. I kicked it closer to the officer. He reached down and saw that I was Sandy Haggard from the picture ID on my license.

I could see that Amber was getting anxious. I thought she might try to run! The officer called out to the other officer's. The one with the gun is Sandy. Let's 10-20; which meant to take Amber into custody.

They started closing in on Amber. Amber was looking back and forth from me to the officer's. I didn't know if she was going to try to charge at me or what, but I wasn't taking my eyes off her nor my hands off my gun!

Then finally an officer had grabbed Amber and placed her in hand cuffs. He was reading her rights to her. He was saying Amber Lynn Newby; you are under arrest for the murder of Todd Adams and attempted murder of Sandy Tucker Haggard. You have the right to remain silent...

Then the officers' voice faded from my ears. I felt someone remove my gun from my hand. It was a female officer.

I watched as the police was leading Amber to the patrol car. I could hear Amber shouting, saying I will get you! I will get out someday! I will kill you!

The officer that had taken my gun from me was still beside me. She was asking me if I was okay. I just collapsed falling toward the ground! The officer caught me to break the fall. All crumpled on the ground, I began crying, praying and thanking God as the officer sat down next to me and comforted me.

After my tears had stopped and it had sunk in that Amber had been captured, I saw the headlights of another car pulling up behind one of the police cars. The police cars flashing blue lights had the area well lit. The approaching vehicle had come from the other direction. It cut across the medium of the highway. Someone quickly came out from the passenger side of the car. Even though it was dark out, I could see that it was Jerry. Someone had returned him to our broken down car.

Jerry came running to me. He grabbed me so tightly. He kept saying he was sorry he had left me alone. He said it was all "his" fault! He was saying if only he'd stayed with me none of this would have happened!

I stopped him from speaking. I looked at him. I smiled. I said it's alright. It's all over. It's not your fault. I told him that Amber had been captured and she would never be able to hurt anyone ever again! I assured him that I wasn't hurt. All things happen for a reason, I said! Amber will burn in hell one day!

I told Jerry that it was only by the grace of God, that I didn't pull that trigger on the gun and shoot Amber. Then I said to Jerry, we have a birthday party to attend!

Again I told Jerry that Amber had been captured..... She was hand cuffed and locked in one of the police cars and would soon be hauled away! I guess by me telling Jerry twice that Amber had been captured, I was trying to make myself believe what I had just saw was real!

The female officer that had caught me when I nearly collapsed had now left me in the arms of Jerry. As I was hugging Jerry, I looked over his shoulder. It was then when I saw those piercing devil like green eyes as they seemed to glow in the dark and they were starring out the window of that police car at me as the car was pulling away. I knew from the look of those green eyes that Amber gave me, if she ever got out, she'd come looking for me again.

An officer on the scene offered to carry Jerry and me to our destination. As we proceeded to go get into the officer's car I saw something out of the corner of my eye. At first I was frightened but when I turned to see what it was that I had saw, a tear came into my eyes.

A little puppy came from nowhere and was crossing the interstate and was about to get ran over. I screamed for Jerry to go and fetch the little pup. He grabbed the little fellow just in time.

As it turned out, the little puppy ends up going home with us. And it wasn't a little fellow! She was a girl pup. Somehow I knew that God had let that puppy find her way to me. God wanted me to know that it was okay to take in a stranger but just to be careful about the strangers I chose. And in a way, I got my miracle child.

Later that night after Jerry and I got home from the birthday party, we were sitting together on the couch with the little puppy between us. We were watching TV as we played with the little pup.

Flashing across the TV screen I saw the words:

BREAKING NEW!!!!

The capture of Amber Lynn Newby has lead Trina Alabama investigators to some good news. The case of the missing person Tammy Jackson has now been reopened. She was presumed dead. With the help of the public eye, matter of fact, with the help of the young teen boy that had found the body of Todd Adams, and Amber's own confession, we have found Tammy. She has been held hostage in an underground cellar of the old house that Amber was thought to have abandoned years ago. Tammy Jackson is weak and hungry and carries a few cuts and bruises, but is alive and being carried to a local hospital.

As I listened to the words as the news reporter was speaking, I saw the news camera crew as they showed live pictures of the old home place and officers were coming out from the underground cellar with Tammy. I had forgotten about the old underground cellar!

The officers were holding Tammy up and they were carrying her to a stretcher. I watched as everything was unfolding! Tammy was already a small petite girl but she looked even thinner on the TV screen! She looked like she'd been beaten pretty badly!

I know Tammy must have fought Amber back otherwise she wouldn't have come out of this alive! Tammy's hot headedness had probably helped save her life. Next I watched as the ambulance drove off with Tammy. Then I heard the news people say:

Stay with us for further updates as they unfold....

Approximately eight months later Amber Lynn Newby was sentenced to die by lethal injection. I had never believed in the death penalty but being that Amber had strayed from the law for so many years for killing her mother and stepfather, killing Todd Adams and kidnapping Tammy, causing Tammy's family so much heart break, along with the horrible acts that she had done to me, and the pain and heartaches she caused everyone that I cared about, I was all for Amber dying by lethal injection.

Who knows what else Amber may have gotten away with throughout the years of her running? I wonder if any of her former employers knew the real Amber. I wonder if her resume' were all fake. I wonder how many other "boyfriends" Amber might have had or friends for that matter.

I watched Amber Lynn Newby die by lethal injection and I didn't shed one tear. I had never hoped for anyone to burn in hell, but with Amber, I knew she would!

The miracles of God have been seen not only by me but by so many others. I hope that in your lifetime you have seen miracles happen.

My friend Tammy makes a full recovery and is reunited with her son and the salon. The state gave the Baker family the property that had belonged to Amber. The young man that found Todd Adams body and led police to the finding of Tammy has been given a substantial reward for his bravery and heroism.

Jerry and I are growing old together. Jerry has gone back to playing his music on the roads, only this time around I travel with him. My health and physical being is very good. We live in his travel bus while on the road. From time to time we come back to Trina Alabama to touch base with friends and check on our home. Our little puppy, we named her Miracle. She has grown older and is now the proud momma of her very own babies. I guess that makes me a grandma and Jerry a pawpaw!

Miracle and her pups travel with us. I play beauty shop with Miracle and her babies. I wash and brush their hair, and sometimes add a bow or two. They love to ride with Jerry and I on the bus. They have their very own little bedroom area. For some reason, Miracle has taken up with Jerry. She has become his baby. She loves to ride in his lap when we travel. The other pups still sleep a lot. You never know, I might start me a mobile pet salon.

As for my days of torture, they are over. There is times that my past comes back to haunt me, but I have learnt to deal with it. God is my savior and my shelter. I live for one day at a time.

Amber is dead and she can never hurt me or any other ever again. But rest assured; there is still plenty of Amber's out there somewhere! Who knows, Amber may have an illegitimate son or daughter that nobody knows about. After all, Amber had disappeared for many years before she was captured. Could be that her child would turn out to be just like her!